GRECO

ALSO BY C. G. COOPER

Corps Justice Novels

Corps Justice (previously titled Back to War)
Council of Patriots
Prime Asset
Presidential Shift
National Burden
Lethal Misconduct
Moral Imperative
Disavowed
Chain of Command
Papal Justice
The Zimmer Doctrine
Sabotage
Liberty Down
Sins of the Father
A Darker Path
The Man from Belarus
Matters of State
Payback
Black Mist
The Algorithm
Breaking Point
Kill Chain

Lone Peak Heroes Novels

The First
The Second

The Third
The Fourth

Daniel Briggs Novels

Adrift
Fallen
Broken
Tested

Tom Greer Novels

A Life Worth Taking
Blood of My Kin

Standalone Novels

To Live
The Warden's Son
The Nicene Cipher
The Next Dawn
Higgins
The Patriot Protocol

The Chronicles of Benjamin Dragon

Benjamin Dragon—Awakening
Benjamin Dragon—Legacy
Benjamin Dragon—Genesis

Corps Justice Short Stories

God-Speed
Running
Chosen

GRECO

A NOVEL

C. G. COOPER

LAKE UNION
PUBLISHING

Text copyright © 2024 by JBD Entertainment, LLC
All rights reserved.

No part of this book may be reproduced, or stored in a retrieval system, or transmitted in any form or by any means, electronic, mechanical, photocopying, recording, or otherwise, without express written permission of the publisher.

Published by Lake Union Publishing, Seattle

www.apub.com

Amazon, the Amazon logo, and Lake Union Publishing are trademarks of Amazon.com, Inc., or its affiliates.

ISBN-13: 9781662525704 (paperback)
ISBN-13: 9781662525698 (digital)

Cover design by Jarrod Taylor
Cover image: © Rekha Gart / ArcAngel; © Nora Carol Photography / Getty;
© Ratana21 / Shutterstock

Printed in the United States of America

To MG. This story is for you. Thanks for letting me into your world. I treasure your friendship more than you know. Keep being your authentic you.

—cgc

Prologue

They call me Greco. Technically, I was born Michael Angelo Greco, if you can believe that. The only two people who call me Michael are my mother and sometimes my little brother, Tommy. Though Tommy calls me everything from Michael to Mike to Mikey, he refuses to call me Greco. Mom and Tommy are two of the stubborn stalwarts in my life, the two people I love the most and yet resent because of that love. But you don't want to hear all the boo-hoos yet. There's plenty of that to come.

As I was saying, I was born Michael Angelo Greco in a little hospital called Saint Mary's in Shiply, Illinois. It's a little Podunk town that used to be something, or could've been something. Depends on who you ask. We're close enough to Chicago for that to be a problem and a connection. More on that later. Back to my birth . . .

I remember asking my mom when I was a kid if we could visit the hospital where I was born, and she said someone had torn it down and put a Safeway in its spot. Then she made the sign of the cross and probably said a Hail Mary for good measure.

Mom clings to the Catholic religion like a wino to his bottle. Mom isn't perfect, but she tries. She really did with me. Although she made me comb my hair and wear clean clothes when I went off to school, inevitably, when I came home, my hair was a mess and my jeans were grass stained. She'd scold me and make me scrub them in the kitchen sink. I got pretty damn good at doing laundry, which probably has something to do with why I like my clothes spick-and-span clean now. One of a few quirks I've picked up along the way.

I'll warn you now: I'm not sure exactly where this story will go. I'll most likely dip back into my early childhood so you can understand who I am and why I did what I did. No excuses. The truth.

Why am I writing this? A couple of reasons. First, I want my kids to know the real story. I want them to know that I was a real guy with real problems and that if you work hard enough and surround yourself with the right people, maybe it'll work out? Second, it was cathartic to get it all on paper, though I'm not sure it'll see the light of day. Maybe I'll read it again in fifty years, laugh at my bad grammar, and cry at the memories. Who knows . . .

You're also probably thinking, Why Michael Angelo, right? Like the painter? Mom liked to say that I was born a saint, and she pretended that she knew Michelangelo's work, though I think it was more because she was trying to get my dad to take her to Rome. Spoiler alert: they never made it to Saint Peter's.

Years later, I would travel to the Sistine Chapel and gaze up at the magnificent work done by my namesake-ish. I still remember the smell as I stood there staring up at that beautiful ceiling, thinking about Michelangelo's work. How many hours of toil? How much love had it taken? How much inner turmoil to accomplish such a feat?

I stood there waiting for some sort of connection; I don't know what I expected. A paintbrush to suddenly appear in my hand? A modern image of David to pop into my head? Well, none of that happened, but peace did—despite all the tourists bustling about me, murmuring in their native tongue, though the caretakers of the chapel kept shushing them.

I heard a rumor that I was named Michael Angelo Greco because Dad lost a bet. Now that one, I believe. Dad lost many bets over his lifetime, though he tried to cover up his losses in any way he could.

About Dad: There are some good memories there. Like tearing down a highway together, holding on for dear life to the Harley-Davidson that he'd borrowed from a friend. We both screamed at the top of our lungs as the world flew by. Mom hit the roof when she heard about it, but that memory of Dad and me is one of the things I go back to when stuff really hits the fan.

I try not to dwell on the bad stuff. Like when I visited his office and saw a picture on his desk with Dad, a woman who was not my mother, and a little kid with messy jet-black hair. When I asked him about it, he said they were friends. I'd later find out it was his second family. Yeah, pretty messed up, like something you see in a dramatic TV miniseries. And I never saw that picture in his office again. Probably because he told me to always call before I visited again.

Inevitably, the shadows come, the habit-forming recollections. The ones that sometimes make me wake up in a cold sweat, feeling under my pillow for the blankie that's no longer there. I kept it through high school, and of course I hid it from my friends. That was a small piece of my childhood that kept me safe when nobody else could.

So yeah, call me Greco, and if you like stories about tattered childhood, crooked family, dirty politics, and football, maybe you'll like mine.

And with that, let's get to the good stuff—the most important, harrowing, stress-filled, depression-inducing, exciting, gravity-bending year of my life. It was my first year in college. It was the year I became a man. It was 1989. It was the year everything changed.

Chapter 1

I pulled up to Jefferson State University in a Yellow taxicab that smelled like day-old pizza. When the cabbie asked if I wanted him to take me all the way to the dorm, I said no. There was a building at the center of the university that was said to have been designed by Thomas Jefferson himself. It was the intersection of campus life: rallies held, parties begun and ended, ten-mile runs completed in a huff and with a thrumming heart.

After I got out of the cab, grabbed my two duffel bags, and paid the taxi driver, I looked up at that building and took in a deep breath. This was a new start for me. No more Podunk town. No more Chicago connections. No more drama. At least that's what I told myself, knowing full well that all those things had come to college with me courtesy of dear old Dad.

I slung a duffel over each shoulder and took the long way to my dorm. It wasn't the official first day of school. Football players were expected to check in two weeks earlier. There was plenty of running and sweating to do before the other students arrived.

Football and academics, I was ready for. I wasn't exactly what you would call an A student, but I did my best, and football did the rest. I was first-team all-state as a middle linebacker. I set three school records and got looks from a handful of college teams, but Jefferson State had been on the top of my list. They played some big-name schools and were said to be on the hunt for a true Division I designation. There was something about being involved at the beginning of a program that fit with where I wanted my life to go. I wanted to build something. Something new. Something bold and heroic.

One of the other reasons that I went to Jefferson State and not to the California college that offered me a full ride was that it was only an hour from home. Give me another life, and I would've moved halfway around the world, but there was still Dad's business to be cared for and my little brother, Tommy, who was still in high school. Because of my mother's irresponsible ways, Tommy was pretty much fending for himself now that I was gone. I gave him a good talking-to before leaving home. I told him exactly what he should be doing each and every day. Get up early. Go for a run. Hit the gym. Come home. Make breakfast for him and Mom. Clean up and get to school on time. Rinse and repeat. Never stop moving. He was a gifted athlete in his own way but lacked the discipline and determination for which I was known.

You see, when I was a freshman in high school, I weighed barely one hundred pounds. I don't know why I went out for the football team (probably to prove something to my dad, I don't remember now), and half the team laughed at me during tryouts. But what they couldn't ignore was that when we went head to head, the scrawny little kid who lived in a single wide kept getting knocked down and kept getting back up. I could barely move the next day, but I still showed up to tryouts. During that week, I proved myself to my high school coach, and I'll be damned if he didn't let me on the team.

I didn't play much that year, mostly when we were up by three touchdowns, but I didn't complain. I rarely do. It's a waste of time, and I hate wasting time.

Like I said, I was tiny. But in the summer between my freshman and sophomore years, I grew. I filled out, worked out, and tried to eat everything I could find, or at least what we could afford. Bouncing on and off food stamps makes finding your next hearty meal tricky. It all depended on whether one of Dad's many business ventures was making hay or flopping, and whether he was in town or away on business. I learned to understand that being away on business was his way of hiding from someone he couldn't pay that month.

Back to my first day. By the time I got to my dorm, I'd worked up a little bit of a sweat, but I felt good. I really felt like I could take over the world. I was a little disappointed that the university was so quiet, but I wasn't about to cry in my Wheaties. I was on a partial scholarship, hoping to get a full scholarship by the end of the year. I'd worked my tail off delivering pizzas for most of high school, mowing lawns when I wasn't working at the pizza shop, and basically doing every odd handyman job I could find. You'd be amazed at what I can fix with a hammer and a screwdriver.

There was a small welcome table at the dorm and a pimple-faced kid I recognized as the team manager holding a clipboard. He looked up and squinted through thick glasses.

"Oh yes, it's Greco, isn't it?" I stuck out my hand, and he ignored it. He pulled out two sets of keys from a cardboard box on the table. "Room 211."

"Thanks," I said, grabbing the keys. "Who am I rooming with?"

"You'll see," he said. He was back to looking at his clipboard. Apparently, he didn't give a damn about freshmen, and that was fine with me.

I went inside, trudged up the stairs, barely squeezing through with my two large duffels, and found room 211. I was glad we were in a normal dorm, not some football dorm. It was coed by floor, and like any red-blooded freshman, I was looking forward to seeing my coed classmates.

My door was unlocked, and when I went inside, I found my new roommate, his clothes scattered all over the room. I cringed. Truth be known, I'm a neat freak.

"Oh hell, man, I didn't hear you come in." He was a Black kid, a full head shorter than I was, with a wide smile, and instantly, I knew we were going to be friends. "The name's Leroy Jackson."

He didn't say Leroy like you typically would, with a long *E*, but with a short *E*. Like L'Roy.

"D back," Leroy said. "From Tampa, Florida. Who are you?"

We shook hands. "Greco," I said. "Middle linebacker."

"Oh hell, I heard about you. You're the head knocker, right?"

I'm pretty sure my face flushed. "I've been known to make some tackles," I said.

"Make some tackles?" Leroy said. "Wasn't it you I saw a film of hitting a guy's helmet clean off? Didn't that thing fly fifty yards?"

"More like two," I said. "And I got suspended for a game for that one."

Leroy whistled. "Then I'm glad we're on the same team, roommate." He shook my hand again. "Say, you don't mind if I already took this side of the room, do you? Gives me a better view of the beautiful ladies walking by."

Yep. We would definitely be good friends, but first, I had to convince my new roommate that his clothes looked better in a drawer than they did on my bed.

Chapter 2

I unpacked and made my bed within fifteen minutes of getting to room 211. It took Leroy another hour to at least get his things in coordinated piles.

He spent more time talking about the girls he had dated and how he really wanted to be a running back. He'd run all four years in high school, but he'd been recruited to be a defensive back.

He was a magnificent storyteller, and I was laughing when the team manager knocked on the door, came inside, and announced he would escort us to lunch in thirty minutes, where we'd meet the rest of the team.

"Hey, Coach, you want to hear a story about how a twenty-foot gator interrupted my sucking-face time on prom night?" Leroy asked, straight faced.

The team manager stood there as I bit my tongue.

"Oh hell, man," Leroy said. "I'll tell you later. Cool?"

He slapped the poor team manager on the arm. The manager shook his head as he left the room.

"Don't worry about that one," Leroy said. "He's a tough nut to crack, but we'll crack him. I promise."

Leroy was all grins and confidence. I felt myself drawn to that. It was new and refreshing, much different from the serious faces of my hometown's laborers. There wasn't much to be happy about there unless the football team was winning on Friday nights.

Thirty minutes later, we were downstairs. We met a handful of our teammates, more freshmen, and more kids from Florida. One of the kids, Pip Harrington, was a kicker from Tallahassee. He reminded me of someone who belonged on the golf team, not the football team. But he had a firm handshake, and I liked how he looked at me straight in the eye, despite the fact that I probably outweighed him two times over.

Pip looked like he came from money, and I liked the way he was put together, creases in his khakis and all. But he didn't appear stuck up. And when he said my name, Greco, he said it with a bit of a southern twang, though it seemed more distinguished than redneck. Besides, I would never call anybody redneck, because my town was probably more redneck than the redneck-est of the southern rednecks.

When we got to the cafeteria, I was starving. I'd been too nervous to eat breakfast, despite the fact that my mother had offered. But she was still drunk from the night before, and I didn't want to take the chance that she would burn the house down to make me breakfast. She was trying to be sweet, trying to be loving, trying to be a mother. But for the past five years, I'd played that role, not her.

"You've got ten minutes to eat," the team manager said. "And then Coach will be here for introductions."

To a kid who'd gone hungry more nights than he'd like to admit, the cafeteria, though a bit run down, had everything an eighteen-year-old football player wanted: carbs, protein, and sugar. I loaded my plate with three hamburgers; the second plate held fries, and the third held four sticky buns.

Everybody else, except for Pip, the kicker from Tallahassee, loaded up too. It was like Christmas for us fat kids. Out of habit I said a silent prayer because I felt bad. I'd left without giving Mom a kiss on the cheek. I couldn't stand it when she smelled like cheap bourbon.

"Lord, thank you for this food. Please watch over Mom and Tommy. Amen." Then I dug in.

A minute later, I looked up to see Leroy with his hand clamped over his mouth.

"What?" I said through a mouth full of food.

"Boy, you better slow down. You're going to choke yourself." I looked around the table at the rest of the freshmen. And sure enough, they were all staring at me. Apparently, I'd put on quite a show.

"Sorry," I said. "A little hungry." I willed myself to slow down, but as I dug into my third burger, from the corner of my eye, I thought I saw Pip looking at me. When I looked up, he went back to his food. I got finished before everyone else, and yes, I polished off all three plates. Growing boy.

Our head coach marched into the cafeteria, trailed by the rest of his coaching staff. He wasn't a big man, but barrel chested, burly, with a scruffy beard and intense eyes. He scanned the room until we all stopped talking. That's when I noticed the upperclassmen still had food on their plates, whereas the freshmen's plates and trays were pretty much wiped clean.

"Gentlemen, for the upperclassmen, welcome back. For you freshmen, welcome to your first day at Jefferson State University." Coach was one of those guys who didn't have to speak loudly to get people's attention, though I'm sure his voice carried for miles. It was something about his gravitas, his natural force, that commanded attention. And here's the kicker. His name was Ulysses S. Grant.

Yes, like the general, like the president. In fact, he looked so uncannily like the American hero that I'd heard whispers that he was the reincarnation of U. S. Grant himself. The only things missing were a chomped cigar and the occasional slip into whiskey. Coach didn't believe in "self-pollution," as he called it.

"Gentlemen, I'll keep this short because there's much to do." There were murmurs from the upperclassmen and confusion on the faces of the freshmen. "I've spoken to each and every one of you and your parents. You know what I expect. You leave your heart and soul out on that field, and I will give you everything that I've got. But if you don't . . . well, you don't want to see what happens when you don't."

The place was dead quiet. You might have heard hoots and hollers from the upperclassmen in any other college. Here, you didn't. Here, Coach Grant ruled with a mallet fist. Not iron, because that would insinuate that he had us each by the balls. It was becoming known across the land that Coach Grant was a new breed of coach, a man of strong will who also knew how to coax the best out of the greenest players.

He'd sat in my single-wide living room that sometimes doubled as my bedroom and told my mother that when he was finished with me, she would be impressed by the man I'd become.

"Like I promised," he said. "That's it for now." Then a little grin spread across his bearded face. "Captain?"

Our starting quarterback, Sam Collins, popped to his feet. He stood at attention, though there was a grin on his face. "Yes, Coach."

"The floor is yours, Captain." And then, like they were on a parade deck, he and the other coaches did an about-face and marched out of the cafeteria. I glanced down at the table and thought I detected a stream of nerves running through the freshman class. I glanced over at the team manager. He was grinning too.

"Gentlemen, as Coach said, welcome to Jefferson State University." Then he clapped his hands together. "Seniors, they're all yours."

That's when the seniors turned on the rest of us and started screaming. And before the first hour of Hell Week was over, every one of the freshmen in my class had deposited that first meal onto the green fields of Jefferson State University. Lucky us.

Chapter 3

I won't bore you with all the details of more puking, sweating, and foul body odors. Hell Week was called that for a reason, but I could also see that the process of tearing freshmen down had its purpose. And though in the beginning it was the seniors yelling at us, ultimately they did every sprint, every push-up, and every pull-up. On Coach Grant's team, everyone felt the same pain, and everyone experienced the same glory. And during Hell Week, everyone had to dig down deep and never, ever quit. We only lost one. To be honest, I had him pegged from the very beginning; he wasn't just soft around the middle. Trust me. We had plenty of guys bigger than him. But the softness in his eyes spoke of a gentler life—a life not riddled with pain—a life unlike mine.

As for me, yeah, it sucked. But the masochistic part of me that made it through my childhood relished the pain. I saw the coaches' appreciative glances and the contented nods from the upperclassmen.

I knew from experience that it was important to be a team player, so when my freshman teammates fell behind, I helped them, egged them on. I pulled and dragged them when I could. I cajoled where needed. I figured out my class's strengths and weaknesses. My roommate, Leroy, for example, could run for days. His legs never seemed to tire, but the sit-ups always got him. Didn't matter that he had a six-pack.

"It's a family curse, man," he would tell me at night. "The Jackson men have fine physiques, but our abs are our weakness."

When we'd get back to the room each night, he'd give me a run-down of what he saw with the team. I kept my own observations to myself. Not that I didn't want to share my thoughts with him, but I was still processing. Our friendship grew quickly, and it was obvious that we would soon be the leaders of our freshman class. There was another player that surprised me—our kicker, Pip Harrington. He looked like a coun-try-club jockey, but he could outrun everyone, including myself, except for Leroy. Plus, he did more pull-ups than everyone but our captain. He never complained, and though he wasn't nearly as strong as the rest of us, he pulled his own weight and more. I wondered if God had given him a bigger body, whether he would have gotten a full-ride scholarship to USC or Notre Dame. He was stoic, whereas Leroy was quick to tell a story.

Pip, Leroy, and I made an unlikely trio, but that's team sports now, isn't it? I've heard it's kinda like the military. You come from all walks of life, and you prove your mettle through physical tasks. For us, the real test would come on the gridiron, though life would give us a bigger test later.

We'd made it to Friday. We ran in formation from the cafeteria, where we had light breakfasts. You still had to eat. Leroy was out front calling cadence. He told me on our second night that he'd gone to military boarding school for two years after getting in a bit of trouble in eighth grade. Something about lighting his English teacher's skirt on fire. (Don't worry. She wasn't hurt.)

Leroy planned to get an officer's commission, and the army had already offered him a scholarship, but he had his eyes on the Marine Corps. Evidently, his grandfather had been somewhat of a trailblazer in the Corps, and Leroy wanted to follow in his footsteps.

When we got to the practice field, we went through what was now routine—fifteen minutes of calisthenics followed by thirty minutes of sprints, too many push-ups to count, and then Leroy's dreaded sit-ups. He groaned as I sat on his feet and wrapped my legs around his.

"Come on, Leroy, you've got this."

He set his jaw and went to work.

"One, two, three, four," I counted.

We were almost at fifty when Coach Grant's whistle blew. I can't explain how you knew it was his whistle. You just did. It probably didn't sound any different in pitch, but it definitely sounded different in intensity.

Everyone stopped what they were doing and looked to the center of the field where he'd been watching. He never wore a hat or sunglasses, no matter how hot or sunny it was. It was like he was daring the sun to burn him.

"Everybody up," he bellowed, and everybody jumped to their feet, and we made a wide circle around him. "I'll spare you the mystery," he said once we were settled. "Congratulations, gentlemen, Hell Week is over."

My class had learned not to say a damn thing until the others had. So when the upperclassmen started cheering, we did too. I saw tears of gladness wetting some eyes, even older guys'. And I'm not embarrassed to say that I was cheering, too, that I felt an emotion I'd never felt. This was beginning to feel like family, and to a guy whose family was more than a little dysfunctional, a new family felt like a gift from Santa Claus.

I felt the tears coming, but when Leroy wrapped an arm around my waist, I bit them back.

"Do you hear that? We're done!" he whispered to me.

"Yeah," I said, struggling to contain my voice.

Coach Grant held up a hand, and we all hushed. "Freshmen, you've each been assigned a big brother. Seniors, when you return to your lockers, you'll find a name, and that's your little brother for the year. In case there's any question, a big brother is not someone you run errands for; you don't buy roses for his girlfriend, you don't clean his dorm room, and you sure as hell don't buy him a case of beer." There were chuckles among the players. It was the first real levity of the week. "The rest of the day is yours, gentlemen. We meet up right here, five a.m. tomorrow." I thought I heard a couple of groans, but nobody said anything out loud. "And seniors, don't forget, before the end of the day, you talk to your little brothers. Am I understood?" The seniors all barked out at once, "Yes, Coach!"

"Excellent. Now, get cleaned up, gentlemen, and have a good day."

Chapter 4

I'm pretty sure the shower I took that morning was the most glorious I'd ever had up to that point. When I returned to my room, Leroy was lying on his bed, still wearing the same clothes he'd worn that morning.

"Leroy, I'm about to give you some truth," I said.

"Send it, brother."

I sat on the edge of his bed, which was, of course, unmade. "Leroy, you stink."

He chuckled. "Yeah, I know." But he didn't move.

"Leroy, you know I love you."

"Yeah, I know that."

"But I've got to be honest—if we're going to be friends, and if we're going to be roommates, you better get your happy ass in that shower. If our room starts to smell like feet—"

"Okay. Okay," he said, slipping from the bed and grabbing his towel and shower kit. "You know, I came to college thinking that my mom wasn't coming with me," he said, but he was smiling.

"Don't make me make you make your bed," I said.

He raised his hands in the air and twirled around. "Okay, Mom. I'm going. I'm going."

I dressed and tidied my side of the room, which was already tidy, but no sense in not giving it another once-over. When Leroy returned, whistling as usual, I had a plan in mind.

"I need to run a couple of errands. Meet you for lunch at noon?"

"You want me to come with you?" Leroy asked.

"Nah, it's boring stuff," I lied.

"Okay, then. Meet you at the cafeteria at noon."

I had a laundry list of things to do that did not include laundry. There was business to be done, and while there was a phone in our room, I needed privacy. Luckily, I'd already scoped out a public telephone. One of those you put quarters in, and it was in a booth where I could close the door and take care of what I needed to take care of.

My first call was home. Tommy picked up on the second ring.

"Yeah," he said.

"Tommy, how have I told you to answer the phone?" I asked.

"Mikey, hey, man. How's college? You got a girlfriend yet? How's the food?"

"Settle down, Casanova," I said. "College is good. We got done with Hell Week today."

"Oh man, how many times did you puke?"

"Three," I said.

"I would've paid money to see that," he said. "How's the rest of the team? You guys going to win this year?"

Jefferson State was coming off a losing year, and Tommy had ribbed me to no end on that one.

"We look good. I'm not sure I'll start, but I think I've got a shot."

The starters at linebacker were impressive, and I'd have a mountain to climb before I could get to their level. They were bigger than me, mostly faster than me, and they knew Coach Grant's system. Most of all, they'd all played together, so they knew what was what.

"How's Mom?" I asked. There was a pause on the other end, and I knew what Tommy was doing. He was thinking about how much he should tell me, so I said, "Just say it."

"She's running around with that guy again, the one who works down at the bait shop."

"Sasquatch with the curly hair?" I asked.

Tommy chuckled. "Yeah."

"He been to the house yet?"

"Not yet, but she wants to introduce me."

I knew the guy and didn't want him anywhere near our house.

"Come up with an excuse. Get creative, will you?"

"Sure, yeah. No problem. Hey, it was great to talk to you, Mikey, but I've got to go see my girlfriends."

"Girlfriends. Plural?" I asked, not surprised.

"Well, sure. They all want me, and I have to pick the winner."

"All right, fine, but make sure your room's cleaned up and that you have dinner on the table when Mom gets home."

"Okay, big brother. Try not to puke too much." He laughed as he hung up the phone.

I shook my head and sorted some more quarters. Then I dialed the number from the piece of paper that I'd stuck in my wallet.

"What?" the person on the other end answered.

"It's Greco."

It sounded like the guy on the other end put his hand over the receiver, and I heard scratching. Then I heard a familiar voice. One of Dad's business associates, a man who'd given me Tootsie Roll Pops when I was a kid.

"Greco, how are you, my boy?" His voice grated in my ears.

"I'm fine." It was hard to be polite.

"How's college?"

"It's fine. We haven't started yet."

"Oh, right, preseason workouts."

He said it like he knew what he was talking about. I wanted to end the call as soon as I could.

"I wanted to check in, see where we stand."

"Where we stand?" the man asked. "Where we stand is that your dead father left a big fat mess."

That big fat mess was the gift I was given at the side of my dad's dying bed. Surrounded by his so-called friends as he took his last breaths thanks to untreated pneumonia, I was told that Dad's associates would be there for me and for my family, but that there were debts to settle first.

I did not say what I wanted to say, which was *Yeah, I know that, you fucking piece of shit.* Instead, I said, "Tell me what I need to do to get things fixed."

He told me, and I made notes on the back of the piece of paper with his number on it. When he finished giving me detailed accounts of my dead father's loose ends, he said, "I've got someone coming by."

My stomach clenched. "There's no need for that," I said.

He chuckled. "Oh, look at Greco. Pretty college boy. Don't worry. It's somebody you know, and they're bringing you a present."

I didn't want a present. Silence fell on the other end, and I didn't know if he'd ended the call.

The voice came again, and amusement tinged every word. "You stay in touch, Greco, you hear? Who knows? Maybe I'll come watch one of your games."

That was the last thing I wanted.

Chapter 5

It was nice to eat lunch without worrying about keeping the food down. Despite my "errands," I was starving.

The cafeteria workers grinned knowingly as the football team collected their heaping helpings of food. Leroy saved me a seat; this time he hadn't picked a long table. It was just the two of us. When I sat down, he looked serious. First, for a second, I thought that maybe he had figured out my secret, but then he said, "I need to talk to you about my big brother."

I relaxed and shoved three french fries in my mouth.

"You already know who your big brother is?"

Leroy nodded, stabbing at his fruit salad absently.

"Well, who is it, Leroy?"

"The biggest son of a bitch on the team," he murmured.

"Coach gave you Wilbur Downs?"

Wilbur Downs was an enormous offensive lineman, and he was pretty much the polar opposite of my roommate. His southern accent was so thick that sometimes you couldn't understand the plays he was calling, but you could sure as hell tell when he was mad at you. He was quick to give the lower classmen a tongue-lashing, and it seemed the only two people he listened to were Coach Grant and the captain.

"My life is over, man," Leroy said. "He's going to kill me. I know it. You tell my mom I did my best, okay?"

"He's not going to kill you, Leroy. Now come on, eat your food." I was hungry but suddenly had to force down the food. I was thinking about who my big brother would be. Maybe there was some sadistic bastard who'd set his eyes on me and wanted to make my freshman year miserable. From the look on Leroy's face, that's exactly how he felt, that his life was now over. But no one approached me during lunch, and thankfully, by the time we finished eating, Leroy was chatting happily again, telling stories, slapping our fellow freshmen on the back.

We decided as a class to take a stroll through town. It wasn't a big town, but there were a few restaurants, a convenience store, and bars, of course. But what we were really looking for were girls. We weren't sex-starved maniacs; we were still kids, but it had been a week, and we were almost men, too, at least in the size of most of our bodies. Leroy was the ringleader, and when he wasn't telling stories along the way, he gave our teammates a good-natured ribbing. Dealing with other people for him was natural. For me, it was a chore.

I'd always felt like there was an instant distance between my peers and me. Maybe it had something to do with the way I was raised. Maybe it had something to do with the fact that I've basically been acting like an adult since I was five. That happens when your dad skips town and you have to ask the landlord for another week to pay the rent or beg the electric company not to shut off your power. But I had a lingering doubt and fear was that I was different, a freak. Maybe I should keep my side of the room a little less tidy to fit in. Maybe I should try to act like Leroy, give people a hard time, kid around. But that wasn't me. Never will be me. I am who I am, and my team would have to accept me for that.

We'd reached town when Pip walked up beside me.

"Penny for your thoughts," he said.

"Thinking about school," I lied.

He gave me that look that told me he knew I was lying. How did he know?

"You got a girlfriend back home?" he asked.

"No."

"What? Did you dump her before you left?"

"Never really got that serious, you know?"

He shook his head. "Greco, I know a lot of things. I know, for example, that my golf handicap is a three. I also know that I can do ten more pull-ups than you. I also know that a guy that looks like you—hair that looks like it should belong to a rock star, chiseled jaw, intense eyes—I know girls go for that shit all day long and thrice on Sundays." I shrugged. "You're not going to tell me, are you?" he asked.

"There's nothing to tell, man. I was always busy. School, football."

I didn't say family. Family always kept me busy.

"Okay, I understand," Pip said. "You don't want to tell me, that's fine."

Then he grabbed me by the elbow and looked me dead in the eyes. The rest of the team walked on as we stood there. "We're going to take over this team, Greco—you, me, Leroy. But in order for that to happen, we need to be honest with each other. You understand?"

I nodded, but I didn't understand. The intensity coming off Pip was unnerving. It was like he could see right through me, and I didn't like it. Didn't like it one bit. "You'll understand, I promise," he said, letting go of my elbow. "Now come on. I think I see a girl who's my type."

I forced out a laugh but let him walk ahead. I have no idea why Pip singled me out.

Chapter 6

A funny thing started happening after my dad died. Well, funny to you, maybe, but not so amusing to me. I started having dreams. Very, very vivid dreams. You know, the kind where you wake up and wonder what's real.

I'm not sure if it was because of the stress of Hell Week or that I was in a new place, but I hadn't had one since arriving at school. Maybe the relief of finishing the hard stuff or the phone call home settled my brain. Maybe it was a combination of the two. Either way, that Friday night, the dreams came again.

This time I was on a boat with my dad. We were cruising along the Chicago River, gazing at the cranes dotting the Chicago skyline. My dad was sipping from his ever-present insulated coffee mug.

"You see that spot with all that trash and overgrown grass right over there? There will be a skyscraper as high as the Empire State Building. You know who's going to own a piece of it? You and me, son," he said.

"How, Dad?"

I was a kid again in my dream, and the world felt big, full of wonder and surprises.

"It's important to have friends, son. But that project right there? I helped Councilman DiMaggio get that piece of land."

"DiMaggio? Like the baseball player?" I asked.

"That's right, son."

Dad was an avid baseball fan. He didn't have a favorite team, but he could rattle off stats from 1937. He would tell me the starting lineup for the Boston Red Sox in 1972. He'd taken me to Cubs games, White Sox games. Hell, we'd even taken a trip out to California on one of those stints when we were living high on the hog. We'd seen the Giants in San Francisco, the Dodgers in LA, and the Padres in San Diego. Those were good memories. Just me and Dad, impervious to what was going on back home. Still, while we were technically on vacation, he'd find a pay phone to make a call. He said he had to be connected with "the business." I'd seen him do it for years. I didn't know any different.

So, there we were, floating down the Chicago River. Dad would've made an excellent tour guide. I would never know whether he knew this stuff for real or was full of shit. But Dad spoke with conviction when he explained how a certain deal was pulled together and how an architect was chosen from Argentina or New York. The way he talked, you would think that it was his city, and it was easy for a kid to believe it was his too. Because that's how Dad was. He was a man of tall tales and taller promises. The reality was the tales kept getting taller, and the promises kept getting broken.

There were times in my life when I didn't see Dad for months or a year at a time. Mom would miss rent, and we'd leave before we were evicted. Mom had it all together back then. Packed us lunches for school and everything. Even volunteered at the church and went to PTO meetings. Whenever we got evicted, Tommy and I would huddle on a cousin's couch and make forts with smelly blankets made by long-dead grandmas. We'd say please and thank you, as Mom told us, so that a surly aunt would feed us. Then Dad would come home with armfuls of gifts like he'd been away exploring the world for us. We were rich for a time, going out to fancy dinners and buying new bikes. Then, things would cycle back to the way they were before. Always scraping. Barely getting by—the money gone. Thirdhand clothes returned.

As a kid, it was hard to understand what Dad was. I just wanted him to be my dad. I didn't get that there was money to be made and the only way Dad knew to make money was to hustle. And boy did he hustle when he needed to.

"This isn't real," I said to Dad in my dream. This was how it always happened. At some point, I knew I was in a dream. I wasn't a kid anymore, and my dad was dead. Not doing underhanded deals in Chicago or Toledo.

"What are you talking about, kiddo? This *is* life." He spread his arms wide, inviting me to the celebration.

"Dad. You're dead." He turned to me slowly, still holding his coffee mug, but his eyes were no longer shining with excitement. They were caved in and dark, and within each were tiny red burning coals, and when he opened his mouth and dribbled out black sludge, I screamed.

Chapter 7

"Greco, Greco. Wake up."

Somebody was shaking me, and when my eyes opened, I saw Leroy standing over me.

"Hey, man, are you okay?" he asked.

I sat up in bed and looked around. When I glanced at the clock, it said 3:14 a.m.

"What? Was I talking in my sleep?" I asked, though I knew what the truth was.

"You must have been dreaming. You screamed. Scared the hell out of me and probably all the ghosts in the graveyard too!"

"I'm sorry," I said.

"Nah, man. No problem. I was scared for you."

I slid off the bed and put my feet on the ground. Something about the solidity of the floor made me feel whole again. I tried to push the image of my demon father's face out of my head. When I reached out to brush some of the hair out of my face, I realized my hair was drenched in sweat.

"I don't think I can go back to sleep. I'm going for a walk," I said.

"You want me to come with you?" Leroy looked worried, and that's the last thing I wanted.

I put on a fake smile and said, "It's fine. Hell, maybe I'll go for a run. Got to get my legs strong enough to keep up with you."

"In your dreams," he said.

That's right. In my dreams, I thought. I dressed quickly and went out the door, and before I was gone, Leroy was already snoring again. The dorm hall lights were on like always, and I laced up my shoes, did a quick stretch, and went outside. Though it was after three in the morning, it was still sticky. Thank you, Illinois summer. I walked for a few blocks and then decided to take my own advice and start running.

By that point, I had stopped trying to decipher my dream. It was a dream. But it was always me and my dad.

Sometimes Tommy was there; sometimes Mom was there. And they didn't all end the same way. There didn't seem to be a lesson, but they seemed to be glued to some specific memory. Now that I thought about it, we had taken a boat on the Chicago River. It was a gleaming boat that looked like it had been plopped in the water for the first time, with no green sludge on the side or anything. Of course it wasn't his, but he played like it was. It was after another couple of months of being away, and he said he wanted to spend some time with me, his Greco.

I ran harder, not wanting to think about Dad, not wanting to think about anything except for the tearing, searing strain in my legs and lungs. Somehow, without planning, I ended up at the football field, not the practice field but the actual game field—the stadium.

I eased to a walk and caught my breath as I walked around the stadium, looking for an open entrance. I could have hopped the fence, but what would happen if I trespassed? I'd probably be arrested, maybe kicked off the team, and no way in hell I would let that happen.

I'd almost made an entire pass around the stadium when a flashlight shined in my direction, blinding me momentarily. "Greco?" the voice asked. I knew who it was immediately.

"Hey, Coach."

"Hell Week's over, you know," he said.

"Yes, sir. I know. I couldn't sleep." I didn't want him to think that I was doing this for the benefit of my football game. I was many things, but I was not a liar. Not for football, at least.

"You know, most of your teammates will be sleeping until two p.m."

"Yes, sir. I know," I said.

He lowered the flashlight and joined me as I walked.

"What about you, Coach? Why are you up so early?"

He shrugged, and I could hear the tiredness in his voice when he said, "Same as you. Can't sleep. How are things at home, Greco? Your mom and little brother okay?"

"Yes, sir. They're fine."

"And how about you, son? How are you doing?"

"I'm feeling strong, Coach. I'm ready to play."

He grunted, and I couldn't make out what that grunt meant. It was something I would come to find with Coach Grant; he kept his emotions close to the vest, like me.

"Since you're up, and I've got some work to do, do you want to check out the field?"

My heart leaped at that. We hadn't been allowed on the field yet, and this felt like a distinct honor. "Yes, sir, if it wouldn't be an imposition."

"Now, why would you think that, Greco? This is your home, at least for the next four years." Then he stopped and looked at me. "If there's anything you ever want to talk about, you know you can come find me, right? My door's always open for my players, even the ones who've graduated."

"Yes, sir," I said. But I never planned on playing that particular card.

"I mean it, son. Freshman year can be lonely. Hell, when I went to school, it was the first time I ever left home. Did you know that?"

"No, sir."

"Cried myself to sleep for the first week. I've got a tight family, and I missed them. I'm not embarrassed to say that. It's okay if you miss yours too."

I didn't want to tell him that Tommy was the only person I missed. The rest of them could all go to hell as far as I was concerned. Yeah, maybe even Mom.

Coach pulled out a set of keys and opened the gate that led to both the field and the coaches' offices.

"Enjoy it, Greco, it won't be just you on the field in a couple of weeks. It'll be your whole team. And I hope to see good things out of you, son."

"Yes, sir. I'll do my best," I said. He walked to his office, and I walked toward the field in awe of its grandeur. The stadium wasn't as big as the University of Tennessee's or as pretty as the hallowed ground of Notre Dame, but it was my field. Mine.

As I stepped out onto the grass, I felt electricity course through my body. This was what I would focus on. This would be my life.

Chapter 8

That Saturday, we focused on one thing and one thing only—having fun. Somebody scrounged up some hoses, and we had a water fight at the dorms. Then came a couple of cans of tennis balls, and we played our own version of war, the tennis balls being the missiles and our arms being the real weapons. We split into two teams. Leroy picked me first. Pip was the other team captain, and as soon as he whistled shrilly, the game was on.

At first, it seemed that we were well matched. I let my teammates hog the balls for a time, but then Leroy found me, after dodging who knows how many missiles, handed me three balls, and said, "No way you're staying out of this, Greco. Go get 'em."

And I did. I beamed three of the other team members in rapid succession, taking them out of the game.

"Holy hell, man," Leroy said. "Where'd you get that arm?"

I shrugged, picked up the balls, and continued my attack. After that, our half of the freshman squad won easily.

"Hey, no fair, man," one of our teammates said. "Nobody said Greco was a ringer."

"I'm not a ringer," I said.

"The hell you're not. What were you, the fast pitch champ of Illinois?"

I'd only pitched one season and hated it. I despised having to go home and ice my shoulder and elbow. But more than anything, I hated baseball because it reminded me of Dad.

"Rematch," Pip said.

"All right, fine. Let's put some money on it," Leroy suggested. I'd come to find out that my roommate liked to bet on everything, from games to who could step on the fewest pavement cracks while running at full speed.

"I'm not paying you any money," Pip said.

"Fine. Losers do the winners' laundry for a week."

Everyone hooted at that, and Leroy pulled me and the rest of the team into a huddle. "All right, boys, you know what we have to do." Everyone looked at me. "Get Greco the ball, every one of them, and make sure he doesn't get hit."

The good news? It was no contest. We won laundry for the week and a bragging right that we would lord over the other freshmen for months to come. I was helping the others gather up the balls and coil up the hoses when someone nudged me. "Hey, Greco. Collins is looking for you."

I looked up and saw our starting quarterback leaning against the building, looking, quite honestly, like he owned the place. My stomach tightened. I knew what this meant. Everyone else had gotten their big brother the day before, but not me. I walked over to Sam, and he greeted me with a "Let's go for a walk, Greco" that made me want to say "Yes, sir." But I said "Okay" instead.

There were no rules about calling the captain "Captain" unless we were on the field. I definitely didn't have to call him, sir, though. I suppose he could have made up that rule if he was going to be my big brother. We must have walked half a mile before he said anything.

"You probably figured out I'm your big brother, right?" I nodded. "Don't worry. Like Coach said, I'm not going to make you wash my underwear or anything like that."

"That's cool," I said, realizing that I sounded very lame when I said it.

"So why middle linebacker?" he asked me.

"What?"

"Why'd you choose to be a linebacker?"

"I don't know. It fit my personality, I guess."

"Coach said you pick up on plays quick, says you're a hard hitter. I haven't seen any of your film. Is he telling the truth? Honest take, Greco."

"I guess," I said. Where was this line of questioning going?

"When I was a freshman, my big brother was a total asshole. He plays for the Chicago Bears now. The only good thing that came out of it is he's riding the bench these days. Always will. It would really piss me off if he was a starter, you know?"

I'd only seen Collins in his official role as team captain. He always seemed so put together, so in control of the situation. Hell, he looked the part. Tell him to hold onto a football in the crook of his arm and smile for the camera, and he could have been in *Sports Illustrated*. But now he seemed like a normal guy.

"I can't make it totally easy for you. You know that, right?"

"Sure, I get it," I said, disappointed that I felt a little disappointed, but what had I expected?

"But listen, if anything happens to you or the other freshmen, you let me know. You understand?"

"Anything like what?" I asked, completely naive at that moment.

He chuckled. "I forget that you're new at this." He pointed in a big circle. "See this place? They say we're here to get a college degree, but hiding underneath the books and the libraries is life. You're going to meet girls, and you're going to date them. You're going to find beer, and you're going to drink it. There's going to be guys who hate you because you're on the football team. You're going to have to learn to deal with all that. But know that you don't have to do it alone. You get a girl knocked up? You come tell me. One of your buddies gets arrested? You come tell me. The worst thing you can do, Greco, is not tell someone. Do you understand?"

"I think so," I said. This was so against how I'd grown up that I didn't really understand. I was used to dealing with everything myself, shoving everything down until it was a disgusting morass inside my gut. Then the bile-ish ooze would come out in anger, usually on the football field when I would cream the other team.

"Tell you what. Lunch is on me. You like pizza?"

"Does the pope wear white?" I asked.

He laughed at that. "Okay, cool. But I get to pick the toppings."

"Deal," I said. But then he asked a question that would change my trajectory at Jefferson State University.

"I watched the end of the battle," he said. "How come you don't play quarterback?"

I thought about lying. But what would that get me? Some of the truth came out.

"I did, for a little bit, my freshman year in high school. I didn't like it." That wasn't completely true. I did like it. I liked it a little too much, and so did my dad. Then I'd gone to my coach and lied. Told him that my arm felt like it was going to fall off, and he had me try out the other positions, and we settled on middle linebacker. Plus, it didn't hurt that I started leading the team in tackles, and I took us to state my freshman year. Nobody asked again whether I wanted to play quarterback because it was assumed that I had been born to play linebacker. But I didn't tell Collins that.

Chapter 9

Reinvigorated by a dreamless night's sleep, I was all skip and bebop when I got back to my room after my morning bathroom routine. The sun had come up, and Leroy was rustling. "Hey," I said, nudging him. "Let's go get some breakfast."

"What time is it?" he asked.

"Six forty-five," I said.

"Six forty-five. What, are you crazy? It's Sunday."

"Hey, man, come on. There's lots to do. Besides, tomorrow it's back to practice. So today . . ."

"Okay, okay," he said, rolling over and casting off his blanket.

"Dude," I said, covering my eyes with my hand.

"What? You never seen another man sleep naked?" Leroy said.

"I've heard of it. I just don't want to see it," I said. I turned around while he dressed. I swear he yawned ten times to convince me that maybe we should go back to bed. But I was too amped up, and for once in my life, I didn't want to be alone.

To his credit, as we left our room, Leroy had perked up, and he was chatting away. "Listen, here's the deal, Greco. I think we should go to the bookstore today."

"Bookstore?" I asked. "That doesn't sound like fun."

"Listen to me. I got the inside scoop. If we get to the bookstore first, we can buy used books. That way, we don't have to pay through the nose to get new books. You hear what I'm saying?"

I'd completely forgotten about books. Then I remembered what I'd heard on my last university tour. Books were expensive. Back then, we had to buy physical books. There was no digital version. A professor could choose any book he wanted, even a $400 whopper that was better served as a doorstop.

On the way to the cafeteria, Leroy bet me that he could eat a bigger pile of pancakes. Don't worry, I took that bet, and I won, while he looked like he was going to hurl when he was finished. To me, it was another day's work. "You sure you want to go to the bookstore?" I asked as we put away our trays and thanked the cafeteria hostess.

"Yeah, man, we got to be the first in line. Another week and the hordes will be here. Let me tell you, my mama didn't skimp and save so I'd have to pay full price for my books." Leroy talked a lot about his family. His father had been disabled most of Leroy's life. There had been some sort of accident in a Louisiana factory. His mother worked three jobs to support her husband and five kids. Every one of the kids chipped in. Leroy said he'd been mowing lawns, washing cars, and taking any odd job he could find since he could remember. Yet another reason I loved the man.

But still, we seemed worlds apart. He came from a loving family; I came from a mixed bag. I didn't doubt that my mother loved me. I knew that my younger brother sometimes resented me because I was older and I told him what to do, but he loved me too. My dad, again, mixed bag, right?

The student bookstore opened at eight, so we had to wait around for a few minutes. But waiting around anywhere with Leroy Jackson was never boring. He made a game out of anything, and today he told me about all his aunts and uncles—which aunts made the best food, which uncles drank the most beer. He told me about the time they went to Gulf Shores, and because it had been paid for by one of his mother's employers, they'd eaten to their hearts' content. "I ate so many fried shrimps that I swear you would've thought I would turn into a shrimp," Leroy said.

"You *are* a shrimp," I said, punching him in the shoulder.

"Screw you, Greco. It's not my fault God gave you the genes of Achilles himself, while I"—he motioned from his head to his toe—"well, I'm pretty damn perfect, too, now, ain't I?"

A woman inside flipped the sign from CLOSED to OPEN, and we were the first ones in. I love the smell of books. To me, libraries have always been a sanctuary, a place away from danger, a place away from the cold.

You see, the Greco boys found out early on that libraries were a great place to sleep overnight. All you had to do was wait until closing time, hide in a good spot, and make sure you were awake for the morning.

In '89, there was no video surveillance in libraries, so that was never a problem. Sometimes we'd find food in the employee lounge. We made it a point to never take anything new, just the extra half sandwich or the banana that looked like it was about to go bad. I always had rules about that. Never steal, never take what we didn't earn. But those nights, when we were cold and hungry, or Mom and Dad were arguing, and I had to take care of my little brother, yeah, I took things, but they were leftover things. Tommy would pick out a book from the kid's section, and I would read it to him while he fell asleep. Though I groaned every time he chose it, I still love *The Little Engine That Could*. Go read that story, and you'll probably understand why.

The lady at the bookstore desk raised tired eyes at us and said, "Can I help you, gentlemen?"

"Yes, ma'am," Leroy said. "Have all the used books been taken yet?" At that, she smiled. It was impossible not to smile at Leroy when he had his charms up.

"You came just in time. I was about to give the last one away," she said.

"Oh, now you're giving me a hard time, aren't you?"

"Would you expect anything less?" she said. It went back and forth like that for a minute, and then she asked, "Why don't you give me your names, and I can pull up your class schedules? Then we can see which books you need." She was very helpful, and I wondered if she gave this much help to the kids when the place was packed.

Leroy got lucky, if you could call it luck. He found plenty of used books. Most of his turned out to be second- or thirdhand. Maybe it was his good karma. But still the total bill was staggering, at least to me, and he tried to wheel and deal a few more bucks before he finally paid. Now, don't tell anyone, but she gave him a discount. He paid with a neat stack of cash he had tucked in his pocket.

I came next, and my bill was almost double his—almost $2,000. "How would you like to pay, young man?" she asked me. I didn't have a stack of cash. Hell, I didn't have a credit card.

"I'm not sure how this works," I said. "I'm on a partial scholarship."

"Academic scholarship?" she asked.

"No, football."

She nodded. "Typically, the way it works is you buy the books now because you're here early, and the team will reimburse you. I'm not sure how much you'll get back, though, for a partial scholarship."

I groaned. I had to buy the books, right?

"I'll tell you what. Why don't we set you up with a student credit account? That way you can pay in installments, and if the football team pays you, you can bring the check right here. How's that work?"

I gulped down my gratitude, feeling embarrassed for how pathetic I felt. "Yes, let's do that, please," I said.

We staggered back to the dorms with arms full of books.

"Hey, don't worry about it, man. At the end of the semester, you can sell some of them back."

"You think so?" I asked.

"Sure. How about you let me handle that? Cool? Just don't go drawing nude pictures of your girlfriend in 'em."

"Cool," I said, though I was anything but. We returned to the dorm and shuffled inside without dropping a single book. My arms ached when we got to our room. Leroy unlocked the door, and when he opened it, there was somebody waiting.

"Lookee here," the uninvited guest said. "It's college boy Greco."

Chapter 10

"Uncle Freddy," I said.

"Here, let me give you a hand with those," he said, but he didn't give me a hand. He gave Leroy a hand.

"Thanks," Leroy said, handing him a stack of his books. That's when I noticed the fax machine sitting on my bed.

"What are you doing here, Uncle Freddy?" I asked.

"What? An uncle can't visit his nephew? Come on, kid, I missed you."

Yeah, right, I thought. Leroy put down his books and offered his hand. "Leroy Jackson, sir."

"Hell, you don't have to call me sir. Call me Freddy. Everyone else does. Easier than saying Manfredo Alexandros Greco, don't ya think?" They shook hands, and I noticed Uncle Freddy had put on more weight. His was the kind of weight that balloons straight out of the stomach, not the sides. He was bald right down the middle and wore a stack of gold chains under his button-down shirt. His pungent cologne filled our room, and I couldn't help feeling that he'd defiled the place. How had he gotten in? Knowing Freddy, he'd either picked the lock or cajoled his way past a university janitor.

"Hey, Leroy, you mind if I have a couple minutes with my nephew? There are some family things we need to discuss."

"Sure, no problem." Leroy must have sensed my unease because he gave me one of those looks like, *Everything cool?* I nodded at him, and Leroy left, closing the door behind him.

"This is a really nice place," Uncle Freddy said. "Sure as hell wish I could have come to a school like this." I knew on good authority that he'd been expelled from high school—something about stealing cans of beans from the cafeteria.

"What's that?" I said, pointing at the fax machine.

"That is your present," he said.

"What am I supposed to do with it?" I asked.

"Let's not get off on the wrong foot, nephew. You know very well what that's for. I see you have a phone, and I've already contacted the phone company and paid for a year of fax service in advance, so you don't have to worry about that. Messages will come through from someone we'll call the broker. It's your job to decipher the messages with this"—he handed me a brand-new Bible—"and close out the business. Don't worry, the broker says they'll start you off easy." He picked up a small duffel bag from the ground and set it on my bed. I fully expected him to pull out bags of drugs. Uncle Freddy was known to dabble and deal. But instead, he pulled out three rolls of fax paper. "These are to get you started. If you need more, that's on you," Uncle Freddy said. "And you never turn it off. You understand?"

"I understand," I said.

"Good." He zipped up the duffel and slung it over his shoulder. "Man, you sure remind me of your pops," he said. I must have cringed because his eyes narrowed. "Your pops was a good man, whether you believe it or not," he said. "But he left some unfinished business, and since you're the man of the house now . . ."

"It's not fair, and you know it," I said.

If it was possible, his eyes went more narrow. "Fair. You want to talk about fair? How 'bout I lost half my net worth when your father died? He made bets his butt couldn't cash. He went out easy. Me? I'm clawing my way back." He stepped forward and poked me in the chest. "And you, you're going to do what's right because if you don't"—his frown turned into a large smile—"I know you will do the right thing, Greco. And do you know why?"

"No, but I bet you'll tell me," I said.

"That's right. I loved your father, but he made plenty of mistakes. Left us all flapping in the wind. But you, you've got big things coming, nephew. So don't let me down. Don't let *us* down."

In any other family, I might've told him to keep an eye on my mom and my brother, but I didn't want him anywhere near them. Especially Tommy. Tommy was the kind of kid who'd believe our uncle and join the ranks of the shady. Besides, Uncle Freddy had a dozen illegitimate kids strewn about Illinois. I ran into one at the grocery store once, and I'll be damned if he didn't look and smell just like his father—poor bastard.

"Is there anything else?" I asked. I wanted him gone.

He looked me up and down, and I could only hope he was jealous. The beer-bellied prick was making me nauseous, what with his sweat and cologne. "Yeah. There's one more thing," he said. He patted me on the cheek the way he knew I hated and said, "Make sure you keep up with your schoolwork." And then he left me staring at the fax machine, the remnants of my father's tangled past.

Chapter 11

The fax machine was up and running by the time Leroy came back.

"What the hell is that?" he asked.

"What does it look like?" I said in return.

"Your uncle brought you a fax machine. What the hell are you? A stockbroker on the side?"

"I wish," I said.

"Hell, man. You think we could send a fax to Japan?"

"No, we can't send a fax to Japan," I snapped.

"Shit, sorry, man. You need some time."

"I'm . . ." I paused, and then my eyes went to the stack of books. "I'm sorry. I don't know how I'm going to pay for all those books. You know?"

He nodded. "It's okay. We'll figure it out. I promise. We're not supposed to get side jobs, but I'm sure we can figure something out." He patted me on the back. "Come on, Greco. Perk up, man."

"Why don't you make your bed, and maybe I will perk up," I said, forcing a smile.

"Shoot," he said. "You keep asking me that, and I'll keep trying. Deal?"

"Deal," I said.

I don't know what I expected from the fax machine. Maybe a slew of faxes to come straight through, but none did. I put my books away. I tidied up my half of the room, then thought about helping Leroy with his half, but didn't someone say that it was better to lead a horse to water?

"Oh hell, man," he said, looking up from the books that lay open on his bed. "I totally forgot to tell you there's going to be a party tonight. Don't worry. I know you like to get to bed early—the party starts early. Now we gotta go."

We had an early practice the next morning, and while my first instinct was to say no, maybe get ahead on some reading, the last thing I wanted to do was sit in my room and stare at that fax machine.

I didn't ask who was throwing the party. I didn't ask where it was. I didn't ask if we were going to dress up or dress down. I just said, "Yes, let's do it."

Leroy clapped his hands together, and for one more afternoon, I was just another normal college student. A kid enjoying his freedom. A few drinks and a few laughs, but a storm was coming, and no amount of drink or laughter could stop it.

Chapter 12

The house where the party was held was small and packed to the gills. Most of our freshman football players were there, and they gave us high fives when we entered, Leroy acting like a celebrity.

"Why don't you get us two beers?" he said. "I'll find us some girls to talk to."

She filled a plastic cup at the keg and looked up when I approached. It was impossible not to stare. Tight jeans, one of those wonderful tube tops that I loved back in the '80s, a perfect amount of cleavage (not too much), brown eyes that I could swim in, hair done up big, but there was an intelligence in her eyes that really got me.

"Here you go," she said, handing me the keg spigot.

"Thanks," I said, trying to act cool but feeling anything but.

"You're gorgeous," she said.

"Excuse me?" I knocked over the stack of plastic cups, and somebody in the room moaned. I picked them up quickly and set them back on the bar.

"Here, let me help you with that," she said. She grabbed two cups and filled them like she'd been bartending since she was born. Minimal foam, though, at that time, I didn't know that was a thing. Now I know it was just like her. It was one of her perfections.

"I'm Sheila," she said.

I had to put down one of the two cups to shake her hand. "Greco," I said.

"Is that your first or your last name?"

I could tell she'd had a little bit to drink but not too much. Her words came easily, and they floated over me like feathers. One of those feathers slipped into my chest and covered my heart.

"Last name," I said. "But everybody calls me that."

"Greco. I like it," she said, and then to my complete and utter surprise, she reached over and ran a hand through my hair. "My God, you do realize most girls would kill for that kind of hair, right?"

My face must have gone beet red.

"I'm sorry. I guess I've had a couple of drinks." She pulled her hand back, her face turning red as well.

"That's okay," I said. "Happens all the time."

She gave me a look. "Does it really?"

I shook my head.

"Trying to sound cool?" she offered.

"Yeah. Well, I should probably get this to my friend. Nice to meet you, Sheila."

I don't know how the words left my mouth.

"Nice to meet you, too, Greco."

I took the beer to Leroy, and he hooted before taking a long slug.

"To my roommate," he said at the top of his lungs.

All the other football players looked at me and bellowed.

"To Greco!"

There was really no reason for this other than the fact that Leroy had said it, but I drank my beer dutifully. I didn't usually drink beer to get drunk, but today it sounded appropriate. With the unannounced visit from Uncle Freddy, the damn fax machine, and the girl surrounded by friends on the other side of the room who I couldn't stop looking at . . . normally, I would've had a beer or two and slipped out the back. I'd perfected the art of the Irish goodbye. But today, I kept filling my drink, and for once, I had fun.

I'm not sure what time it was, but if it was possible, even more people were there now. It was still summer, so it wasn't dark out. I needed fresh air, so I went outside and told myself that a few drinks were fine, but going over the top would be plain stupid. I had to remember we had football practice the next day.

When I stepped out onto the deck, she was there.

"Hello again," she said.

"Hello," I said. "I'm sorry. Did you want privacy?"

"Privacy? Why would I want privacy? I'm at a party."

"Yeah, but you're standing out here by yourself."

"I don't live here, Greco. Come on out."

I walked up next to her, and a passing breeze gave me the first whiff of her perfume. It was intoxicating, more so than the beer. It slapped me in the face and made my blood bubble in the most curious way.

"Having fun?" Sheila asked.

"Yeah, it's good to be away from home."

"You don't like home?" she asked.

I just shrugged.

"You're a freshman," she said. Not in a snobby way, just matter of fact.

"Yep, got here a week ago."

"And you're on the football team."

"How did you know that?" I asked.

"I saw who you're here with. It wasn't hard to crack the case."

"What about you?" I ask. "Senior?"

"Grad student," Sheila said, sipping her beer. This made her more interesting.

"What are you studying?" I asked.

"Psychology."

"Great. You're not going to psychoanalyze me now, are you?"

"Why? Do you want me to?"

At that moment, I should've said *Yes, you can do anything you want to me*. But I took a sip of my beer instead.

"Are you hungry?" she asked.

I was always hungry. "Sure. I guess I could eat."

Was this girl asking me out? There's no way. She was at least four years older than me, drop-dead gorgeous, obviously way smarter, so I must have had too much beer.

"I'm one hell of a cook," Sheila said, "and I would like some pasta and clam sauce. What do you say?"

I wanted to look around and see if she was talking to someone else. "Um, sure," I said unsteadily. I set my beer on the railing, needing the support of the wood under my hand.

She grabbed my hand and pulled me away from the railing. "Come on, I won't bite. I promise."

Chapter 13

We didn't talk much as we walked, and it made me think that maybe Sheila was reconsidering her offer. I expected at any moment that she would let go of my hand and ditch me, but she didn't, and her hand in mine felt natural and amazing.

We walked a way I'd never gone, down a private road and up a hill, and when we got to the top of the hill, there was a house, the likes of which I had never seen. There were too many windows to count. It was modern, expansive, and beautiful.

"What is this place?" I asked.

"It's home. Welcome."

"You live here?"

She nodded and pulled me forward, unlocking the front door and then unveiling the most beautiful house I'd ever been in.

First, you have to remember that my standards weren't very high. Every place I'd ever lived in was run down: chipped paint, nicked doors, and broken pipes. This was . . . it smelled new. Everything was tastefully decorated and obviously expensive: glass shelving, marble countertops, tasteful knickknacks. I was so entranced by the spectacle that I didn't notice Sheila let go of my hand and walk ahead.

"Give yourself a tour if you'd like. I'll be in the kitchen getting started on dinner."

Walking through a stranger's house felt rude, so instead, I followed her to the kitchen, which was as big as a restaurant. Before she started rooting around in the pantry and the shelves, Sheila turned on some music. I don't remember what it was, but I think it was Bon Jovi. The guys back home would have killed me for admitting it, but after that, Bon Jovi became my favorite group. Sheila loved the band.

"Is there anything I can do to help?" I asked.

"Do you know how to chop garlic?"

"I can figure it out," I said.

She showed me how to do it, and though I was far less skilled than Sheila, I figured it out.

"Can you grab a bottle of wine?"

"Sure. Where is it?" I asked.

"Go back down the stairs we came in on and down one more flight. There's a hallway on the lower level. Go to the end, open the door, and pick whatever you want."

The only wine I'd ever experienced was Carlo Rossi in those huge glass jugs, Mom's favorite. I went down both flights of stairs, down the long hallway, and found the door. There was a sign on it that said CHOOSE WISELY. I opened the door, and the smell of cedar floated over me. I flipped on the light switch and took a quick breath: rows and rows of wine bottles, some covered in dust, others newly purchased. I didn't know where to start. I stayed away from the ones covered in dust, figuring those were old and expensive. I picked one with a pretty label of a woman dancing in watercolor. I turned off the light and went back upstairs.

"I hope this is okay," I said, handing it to Sheila. She looked at the label, nodded, and said, "Good taste. The wine opener is in the last drawer at the end of the counter."

I found what I thought was a wine opener. When I held it up, she shook her head. "It's the one with a corkscrew on it."

Embarrassed, I found the right one that I now know is a wine key, but I didn't know how to use it.

"Have you ever opened a bottle of wine before?" she asked.

I shook my head and held out the bottle and opener. "Here."

She rinsed and dried her hands, took the bottle and the wine key, and showed me how to pierce the wrapper, peel it off, stick the corkscrew into the cork, twist it all the way down, set whatever that metal thingy's called, and then pry it open. The cork came out with a pop, and Sheila sniffed the end of the cork.

"Why don't you pour us each a glass? Let them sit out and breathe for a minute."

I found the wine glasses and poured what I thought was an appropriate but not too forward amount. Then I watched her cook. If it were possible, she was more beautiful cooking. Before long, she presented two plates of linguini with clam sauce. It was light, tasty, and delicious. I was almost finished when I looked up and saw her smiling at me. She'd barely eaten anything.

"Do you always eat that fast?" she asked with a smile.

I put my fork down. "Sorry, habit, I guess."

"It's okay; I'm flattered. Here, take mine." She pushed her pasta across the table.

"I can't eat your food," I said.

"It's okay; I'm not that hungry." She sipped her wine and watched as I took more careful spins of the pasta and slurped them down.

"You should be a chef," I said.

"I've thought about it. I waited tables for a while, learned from the chefs in the back. They're the ones who really run the restaurant, you know?"

I didn't know, but I nodded anyway. There were a couple of bites left, and I pointed. She shook her head, so I finished the pasta and wiped my mouth. I hadn't had any of the wine, and when I took a sip, I knew it was good. Better than good. This was another world.

"What about dessert? Do you like dessert?" she asked.

"Sure. What guy doesn't like dessert?" I asked.

"Maybe later."

Then she stood up from the table and offered me her hand. I stood up and took it. I figured this was her telling me it was time to go, that she loved cooking for me, and that she was still laughing inside from watching me eat her food. I knew grad students didn't cavort with freshmen. Instead, she asked, "Are you a virgin?"

Holy hell, did I get tongue tied on that one! "No," I said.

"Do you have a girlfriend?" she asked.

"No. I mean, I did, but nothing serious."

"Did you break up with her before you came to college?"

"It was before that." Truth was, I'd never had a serious girlfriend. The only one, I guess you could say, was Angie Napolitano. During my tenth-grade year, she pursued me, and I found out pretty quickly that she wanted to get pregnant and married as soon as possible. You know there's an ulterior motive when the sex becomes stale. So I said goodbye, and she wailed for weeks.

"Do you think I'm pretty?" Sheila asked.

"Are you kidding? You're the most beautiful girl I've ever talked to," I blurted out, and I actually clapped a hand over my mouth after saying it. Sheila laughed, but she wasn't laughing at me. I saw how her cheeks flushed, and she hadn't let go of my hand.

"What time do you have practice tomorrow?"

"Seven a.m.," I was barely able to say through my thickened tongue.

"Good, then I can make you breakfast too." And then she pulled me toward the bedroom, my leaden feet barely able to keep up.

Chapter 14

I woke up to someone running their hand through my hair. When I opened my eyes, I saw that it was Sheila. Her lipstick was no longer there, and most of her makeup had been wiped away. She was still beautiful.

"Good morning," I said.

"Good morning, gorgeous," she said to me. To that, I had nothing to say.

"Are you hungry?" she asked. At that, my stomach growled. "Stupid question, right? Football players are always hungry."

"You've got us all figured out, don't you?"

"Not really," she said.

I loved how she ran her hand through my hair slowly. "Have you ever had breakfast in bed?" she asked.

I thought about that and wasn't about to tell her. Sure, I'd had plenty of breakfasts in bed, if bed meant sleeping on the floor in the corner of a library, or on a cousin's couch, or worse, huddled in the back of the dumpster trying to keep warm.

"No, I never have," I said.

"Good." She didn't spring up out of the bed, and she didn't stop stroking my hair. Instead, she leaned in and whispered, "Dessert first, and then breakfast."

After "dessert," Sheila disappeared to the kitchen. I ran to the bathroom, borrowed her toothbrush, brushed my teeth, made sure I looked somewhat presentable, then jumped back in bed. A few minutes later, she reappeared, balancing a tray ladened with a cup of coffee, orange juice, toast, bacon, and eggs.

"I didn't know if you liked orange juice or coffee."

"I'll take either," I said. I glanced at the clock. It was 6:15 a.m.

"Don't worry, I can give you a ride back to the dorm to get changed, and then if you want, I can give you a ride to the field."

"A ride to the dorm is fine," I said.

She sat down with the tray and looked at me. "What? Are you embarrassed with me already?"

"Sheila, it's not like that, it's . . . "

"I'm kidding." She leaned over and kissed me on the lips. "I've got work to do."

She watched me eat as she sipped the coffee. When I finished the orange juice, she handed me her coffee mug. It would become our routine, sharing a cup of coffee, and it was one of the most endearing things we did. Thinking about it now, it still brings pangs to my heart.

"Do you practice all week?" she asked.

I wiped my mouth with a napkin and nodded. "Two a day—a couple of hours starting at seven every morning, and then four hours of light practice and film in the afternoon."

"What about nights? Are you on curfew?" I thought I knew what she was hinting at, and I blushed. "I can see it's easy to get you going," she said, leaning over and then kissing me again. I loved how she kissed me, soft but yearning. I had to remind myself that she had a few years on me, and this was probably her routine.

But I didn't want to think about that, not now. It had been a perfect night and even more perfect morning.

That's when I asked, "Did I say anything when I was asleep?"

She shook her head. "No, why?"

I didn't say it out loud, but it was only the second night after Hell Week I hadn't had a nightmare—that my father hadn't visited me and scared me out of my socks.

"Nothing, I sometimes talk in my sleep, is all. I didn't want to scare you."

"Greco, one thing you'll learn about me is there's not much that can scare me."

"You sound pretty sure about that," I said.

She leaned in and kissed me again. I wanted nothing more than to hold her, but when I reached over to pull her to me, she moved away.

"Uh-uh, we've got to get you to practice."

She disappeared into the walk-in closet, and I slipped into my clothes. When she reappeared, she was wearing a pair of cutoff jeans and a T-shirt with flip-flops.

"Wow," I said.

"What?"

"Nothing."

But I should have told her then—I should have told her many times after—how beautiful she was, how amazing she was, how perfect she was in this imperfect world, but I didn't because I was a coward.

Instead, I gulped down the words and followed her to the garage, where a convertible Mercedes waited.

Again, my mouth ran away from me. "Geez, what kind of rich are you anyway?"

"You're not supposed to ask rich people about being rich, Greco." But she wasn't scolding me. She was teasing me. "And besides, my parents are rich, not me."

"I don't know, this looks like it's all yours." I ran my fingers along the car's perfect fender.

"I'm an only child, and there's only so many things you can buy. Besides, when my parents are in town, they stay in this house."

"You get along with your folks?" I asked as she pulled out of the garage.

"Most of the time."

I didn't press.

"What about you?" she asked.

"My dad's dead." Something crossed her face, but at the time, I didn't understand. "It's complicated with my mom, you know?" How could I explain that my mom, once pretty and put together, was now a stumbling drunk?

"I do know." She reached over and grabbed my hand and squeezed it. I was pretty sure in that moment that anything could happen to me and all she would have to do was reach over, grab my hand, and squeeze it, and everything would be okay.

But she needed that hand to drive because Sheila liked to drive fast; and because the Mercedes was manual, she needed both hands to tear us through town, screaming around corners, laughing as her hair streamed back with the wind, and I laughed along with her, wishing that this morning would never end.

Chapter 15

Leroy snapped me with his towel as I stepped out of the shower.

"You're going to tell me everything about what happened last night," he said.

We'd finished our first practice of the day, and he'd been throwing me looks all morning.

"There is nothing to tell," I said nonchalantly, strolling to my locker and digging out some clean clothes.

"The hell there's nothing to tell," Leroy said. "Come on, spill it. I saw you leave with that girl. Who is she? You going to see her again? What's she like?"

"You want me to stand here naked and tell you, or do you want me to put on some clothes and then tell you?"

He made a gesture with his hands, like, *Hurry up and get dressed so we can talk about this.*

As we walked back to the dorm, I told Leroy everything that happened. Well, not everything. Not how I felt about Sheila. He'd probably think it was stupid that I was falling for someone so quickly. And it was stupid, wasn't it?

"Dang, man, you're barely here a week, and you're already picking up an older lady." He whistled.

"I did not pick her up," I said.

"Right, right," he agreed. "She picked you up. That makes it better."

"Look, I'd appreciate it if you didn't spread this around, okay?"

"Who do you think I am, the rumor king? I'm your pal, right?"

We'd only known each other for a week. I knew Leroy liked to talk, but I also knew I could trust him. He wouldn't talk about things that I told him not to talk about. He would come to keep my secrets, and for that, there was no way I could repay him.

"Well then, when do I get to meet Ms. Wonderful?" he asked.

"I don't know. I didn't get her number."

He slapped me on the arm. "Come on, man. What are you, an amateur?"

I shrugged. Yes, I was. I didn't know what the hell I was doing. I held no illusions that I had any kind of sway or power over anyone.

Leroy kept peppering me with questions about Sheila, and I answered the best I could. We got back to our room, and I felt like he had had his fill.

He walked in first, then pointed to the fax machine. "Looks like you've got your first order."

He'd been giving me a hard time, since the fax machine arrived, that I was running some kind of business on the side. If he had only known at the time, he might have asked for a new roommate. There was paper sticking out of the machine.

"I don't think it's working, man," he said, tearing it off. "It's all gibberish."

He handed me the sheet of paper. Sure enough, it looked like a bunch of mismatched words, but I knew better. I had the key. I folded it up and shoved it inside my pocket.

"That's weird," I said, but I knew it was only the first task of many. My father's open-ended affairs hung over me as I tried to be a normal college student. But as the next few weeks would show, my old life clung to me like a skeleton's gnarly knuckles. Though I tried to shake them off, there they were, digging deeper and deeper.

When Leroy left for lunch, I lied and said I wasn't hungry. I pulled out the Bible that Uncle Freddy had left me, the book that would decipher the coded fax.

Right there, I did as instructed and wrote down the unscrambled notes, word for word, making sure that I hadn't missed a single letter. I'd destroy the paper when finished, like I'd been told.

Chapter 16

We'd wrapped the final practice of the summer. The other students started trickling in that afternoon, and the morning after, the flood would begin. The team was brimming with excitement as it crowded around Coach in the middle of the practice field.

Sam Collins called out, "Team on three. One, two, three," and we all yelled out, "Team!"

"Take a knee, gentlemen," Coach Grant said.

We all went down to one knee, putting arms around those next to us.

"If there was something specific you need to be working on, I've singled you out by now. In the coming weeks, we play for keeps. We open on the road, and I expect each and every one of you to have your studies on lockdown. Have fun. This is still college. I know that. I'm not too old to forget, but I expect you to stay out of trouble. Keep each other out of trouble. If you need help with your studies, ask your professors first. Find a friend who can help you, but before it becomes a problem, before you're put on probation, make sure I know. The last thing we want is a surprise. Am I understood?"

"Yes, Coach!" we all yelled.

"Good. Now, if you'll all bow your heads, I'll lead us out in prayer." We bowed our heads in unison. "Father, watch over this team as we head into a new season. Help them become brothers on and off the field. Help them watch out for one another, make lifelong friendships, to understand that the soul of the man is what's truly important, but that the physical efforts that he gives in service of his team are how we come together. Thank you for bringing us together, Father. In your name, we pray, amen."

"Amen," we all repeated.

The older guys on the team broke off into their cliques. We freshmen were in charge of gathering and stowing gear. We were instructed by the upperclassmen on what was expected for normal practices starting that following Monday after school.

When we were done putting everything away, the team manager found me and said, "Coach wants to see you, Greco," and then walked away.

Coach Grant was in his office talking to Sam Collins. They both went quiet when I entered.

"You wanted to see me, Coach?" I asked.

"Greco." I expected Collins to leave, but he stood to the side watching. "I was talking to Sam, and he said you're keeping something from me."

"Coach?"

He stared at me for what seemed like ages.

"You like playing on the line, Greco?"

"Yes, sir."

"You think you can beat the starters this season?"

"I'll try my best, Coach," I said, wondering where this line of questioning was going. As far as I knew, I was the only one who was pulled into Coach's office today.

Coach and Sam shared a look. Coach exhaled. "We've got a problem, Greco." It felt like the other shoe was about to drop on everything that was good in my life.

"Yes, Coach?" I asked.

"Our third-string quarterback is going home."

"Going home, sir?"

"He has to drop out of college. His mother's sick, and I don't blame him."

"I'm sorry, Coach. Is there anything I can do?"

"We'll get to that in a second, Greco. Sam, you want to tell him the rest?"

"Yes, Coach." Sam walked forward and put his hand on the desk. "You know Ted, don't you, Greco?"

"You mean Ted Bucci?"

Ted Bucci was our backup quarterback. I think he was from somewhere around Canton, Ohio. He looked like a steel worker with a dead gaze and strong hands. He was unflappable on the line and barely winced when he got tackled.

"Ted's had three knee surgeries."

"I didn't know that," I said.

"Nobody knows that except you, me, and Coach, and Ted, of course."

"I'm sorry, Coach, but I don't see what this has to do with me," I said.

Coach Grant nodded at Sam. "You told me. Go ahead and tell him."

"I told Coach that you've got an arm. I think we should test you out. You could be my backup until we find someone else."

"I can't do that," I said without hesitation; the mire that was the bile in my throat threatened to reveal itself.

"Why not?" Coach asked.

"I'm not a quarterback, Coach. I like busting through a line. I like yanking people down by the ankles. I like making open field tackles. All that quarterback stuff? I can't do it."

"Look at me, son," he said.

I didn't realize I'd been looking at my hands. I looked up.

"Some men are born to greatness, Greco. That's a small minority. Others are called to it. Now, I'm not going to say you'll end up being a

Hall of Fame quarterback, but your team needs you, and right now our defensive line is strong. Where we need help is slinging the football."

I wanted to come up with all sorts of excuses. I wanted to tell them that there wouldn't be time for me to learn the plays, but that was ridiculous, of course. We learned new plays all the time. I'd learned almost an entire playbook since coming to school. But this was different. This was reading defenses. This was taking the helm. And most of all, adding another burden that I didn't think I could carry.

Sam put his hand on my shoulder. His grin was deep in confidence. I envied him. "Look, Greco, I don't plan on getting hurt. So worst case, you come in after I've given us a huge lead."

"It's not a done deal yet," Coach said. "You still have to show me what you've got. What do you say, Greco? Will you at least give it a shot?"

I did not need this added chain around my neck. But then he tipped me over the edge by saying, "If you say yes, and you make it, I'll give you a full scholarship."

One thing that I always understood was when the door of opportunity cracked open, you bust your way through. Maybe I'd gotten that from my dad. Maybe I'd been born with it. But this was opportunity, and nerves be damned. I looked straight at the coach and said, "Yes, sir. I'll give it a try," knowing full well that I would earn that spot. Getting a full ride and getting a degree meant I would never have to go home. I could be my own man and leave the old memories to history. Time to forge a new destiny of my own.

Chapter 17

If you've never been to college, I can't completely explain the excitement when school fills up in those first days: new faces, new friends, so many conversations—the excitement is palpable. In those early days, it felt like an unlimited opportunity to start over, and I tried to sink into that feeling. Again, I was lucky I had Leroy. He dragged me from room to room, where we met each and every resident of our dorm. He was like a guy running for mayor. Only Leroy never had a fake smile. It was all genuine, and he loved meeting new people. Perhaps one day, Leroy would run for office, but I hoped he wouldn't. I expected the spirit that he had in those days would stay with him forever; it helped keep my spirits high.

The first day of classes was exhilarating. In high school, I did okay without having to try. The difference with college was most everybody wanted to be there. They wanted to learn. They wanted to earn a degree. They weren't like some of my old friends from high school who showed up because they had to. After all, if they didn't, either their parents would tar and feather them or they'd be thrown in juvie. I'd heard one former high school teammate was already locked up. Yet another reason to never go home.

On top of the classes and the atmosphere of kindness and excitement, I received at least two faxes every day. I deciphered them in private, sometimes in a bathroom stall, sometimes in the library. Each situation, I handled as best I could. Sometimes it was a phone call telling so-and-so owner of so-and-so parcel that I was my father's son and that any interest in a certain parcel should be given to someone—the person whose name I'd been given on the fax. I knew they would get harder as whoever was pulling the strings and sending me the faxes went down his list of what my father owed. Keep in mind, there was no way I could verify any of it. I either went along, or bad things would happen to me and my family. Too bad Dad hadn't left me a to-do list because at least then I've could've ticked off each one and seen how far I was from finishing.

I tried not to think about that when I went to class. I listened and took the best notes I could. You wouldn't believe the amount of reading I had to do when I wasn't in class. I knew right away that I'd picked at least two classes because they sounded cool, not because I'd done any research into them. I thought about dropping both, and I could have used my position as a football player to get them switched, but when I looked into it, it wouldn't have worked out. What with practice and games, the selection of classes that I could take was limited.

Leroy, it turned out, was not only at complete ease with people, but he was also one of the most studious students I'd ever met. He sat in his messy half of the room and barely said a word as he plunged into his homework. Whereas I felt like I was falling behind, he was jumping ahead. When he was finished, he would jump up and say, "Come on, let's go see some people."

I never knew who those people would be, and truth be told, I didn't think he did either. But he dragged me along, and sure enough, he knew almost everybody by name by now, and if he didn't, he would ask, and he would immediately put them at ease, making them feel like long-lost friends.

Our first game was coming that Saturday, and at that week's practice, Coach put me with Sam and watched us toss the football back and forth. We started with short passes that kept getting longer. Coach wanted to see how accurate I was and how far I could throw, and I surprised myself. I was rusty, and it took some time, but by the end of that practice, it was rather obvious that my arm was stronger than Sam's. Sure, his accuracy was better. Sure, he knew all the plays. But there was some talent under my hood, and I was more than a little proud when both Sam and Coach Grant told me I had potential. Just like that, I was torn off the defensive line and thrown in the second slot behind Sam.

On top of my schoolwork, I had to learn a quarterback's playbook. Fun. Sam coached me through it, told me the plays I absolutely had to know and that the rest we'd learn along the way. He was a good mentor and would later go on to coach football in the NFL. He had the mind of a wartime tactician and walked me through how to read a defense. Behind him, it would be a fun season to play. Behind him, I knew I would learn the ins and outs of what it meant to be a real quarterback. I only hoped I could pick up some of his calm under pressure. As a linebacker, I channeled my nerves into smashing and tackling. As a quarterback, I'd have to learn to sit in the pocket and wait for the slathering horde to crush my bones.

The good news? I picked up Sam's QB lessons quickly. I let myself relish that for a bit, but then, inevitably, I'd have to go back to my homework or I'd get a fax. I was doing triple duty, and I had no idea how long I could keep it up. And my funds were dwindling fast. It turned out that the money that I had spent on the books was not going to be reimbursed. Some loophole that partial-scholarship players got roped into. The next semester, everything would be paid for, but until then, I would have to fend for myself.

I had to find a job. And once again, Leroy came in handy. He got us applications to work at the cafeteria, cleaning dishes. I barely said three words during the interview with the surly cafeteria matron, but Leroy did get a smile out of her. "She reminds me of my grandma," Leroy said as we left our new workplace, aprons in hand. "So don't mess this up, Greco."

So yeah, it was a busy first week, and our first game was coming. If I thought I was overwhelmed then, I sure had a hell of a surprise coming. Did I mention I hadn't heard from Sheila again? Add that to the list of things going against me.

Chapter 18

Our first game of the season was against a tiny school called Pinkerton College. It was a two-hour bus ride, and I'm not ashamed to admit that I was shaking the entire time. What would happen if Sam got knocked out? What would happen if they gave me the football and made me run the offense? Sure, I knew the plays. Sure, I'd had some reps, but game time was different than practice.

By the end of the first quarter, I told myself that I shouldn't have worried. We were up 21–0. Sam had thrown two touchdowns and run in for a third. It was easy rolling.

But then, in the second quarter, the heavens opened up and the grass field turned to mush. By the time we hit the locker room at halftime, we were up 28–21 and covered in muck. Coach Grant kept his halftime speech short, but I saw in his eyes what Union troops must have seen in General Grant: pure calm and resolve.

"You know your parts. Now play them," Coach Grant said. "Go out there and win." There was no "One, two, three, team." Just grim faces to match our coach. All the starters and those who had been subbed in and out were slathered in mud. I can imagine some were thinking that it was like being a kid again, finding the deepest mudhole and tackling each other for the fun of it.

But I'd seen the light come on in the Pinkerton College players' eyes. They knew they had our number, and they had nothing to lose. They'd only won one game the last season. There was only one way to go, and that was up. What better way to rack up their first win than a knock against us, the up-and-coming Jefferson State?

The third quarter was a muddy brawl. No one scored, though we tried three field goals and missed every one. Both sides were exhausted, but no one was giving up. It was impossible for either team to find firm footing. You planted a foot, and it slipped out from under you. These days, a game like that would probably be postponed, but not in 1989. No. Unless there were lightning strikes on the field, you kept playing. No one wanted to quit.

Sam took the team out at the beginning of the fourth quarter and did a masterful job orchestrating a run down the field. Another score despite the rain pounding down, players slipping and sliding, missed or shrugged-off tackles. But when we kicked the ball off to Pinkerton College, the tides turned and a disaster happened.

They ran it back for a touchdown, then kicked the ball off, and our returner, a normally reliable guy from Oklahoma, fumbled. Pinkerton College didn't let him get away with it. They were all over him and the ball, and they came up with it, hooting and hollering, covered in mud and blood. It was a grind to the end zone, but they made it there, scoring on a one-yard run and missing their extra point. Now they were down by one.

I couldn't hear what Sam was telling the offense, but when they ran out onto the field, I could see the taut determination. We were not going to let our opponents win. Slowly, methodically, we took two yards here, four yards there. Then a first down. Sam completed a pass that was bobbled, but he hugged to the ground, covered in mud. The referees were working overtime, trying to keep the ball wiped down, but it was impossible. The minutes ticked by as our team slogged down the field, one first down at a time.

That was when I got to see Sam Collins's true greatness, the poise under pressure. His feet would slip, and he wouldn't think twice. He'd flick the ball to a running back, leading the way and blocking the opposing line. He was completely in his element.

We were on Pinkerton's twenty-two yard line. I could see what was about to happen. I heard Coach make the call. We were going for the end zone, but something happened at the line. Sam almost fumbled the ball and didn't have enough time to drop back and let the ball fly, even though we had two men already in the end zone, wide open. I couldn't see from Sam's vantage point, so it was impossible to say whether he had an open shot. He ran it instead, his offensive line falling into place as he shouted for their support, and they did their best for their leader. Across the twenty, he stepped to the eighteen, the fifteen, down to the ten.

Big Wilbur Downs, the offensive lineman and Leroy's "big brother," who'd barely said two words to my roommate, charged like an elephant. A lucky hit happened for Pinkerton College. Something that should have been a call. It took Wilbur's legs out, and like a crashing wet redwood, he succumbed with a bellow, but not into the mud—not yet—crashing down into Sam.

I didn't hear the break, but I saw our quarterback crumble, and everyone in the stadium heard Sam's scream. For a moment, all you could hear was the scream, the rain pounding down, trying to mask the anguish. Our coaching staff ran onto the field, though Coach Grant walked like he always did. Never in a hurry, always with purpose.

The picture that would grace the news the next day was of Wilbur Downs, the big, tough offensive lineman, helmet off, cradling the head of his quarterback, who was still holding the football. Wilbur was crying, and Sam was screaming. The Pinkerton College medical staff was fast. They somehow pried Wilbur's hands from Sam, hoisted him onto a stretcher, and covered him with a tarp so that the crowd couldn't see our quarterback's leg bent in an awkward angle. The refs let him keep the football, which he took with him to the hospital.

I just stood there, slack jawed, and didn't even realize when Coach Grant was talking to me.

"Greco," he said, grabbing the front of my jersey.

"Yes, Coach?"

"You're in, son." That's all he said. No grand speeches. No *Go get them, boy. You're going to do it for the Gipper.* No. It was "You're in," and that's when I was thrown into the muddy gauntlet of Pinkerton football.

Chapter 19

I could barely mouth the words for the play I'd been given. I had to repeat them three times. The first play was a mess. I bobbled the ball from my center, fell back onto my butt, and barely got to my feet, but was still throttled six yards behind the line.

I glanced at the clock. Two minutes, eleven seconds. I let the clock run down to two minutes. Two-minute warning. The refs blew their whistles, and each team went to their sideline. It wasn't Coach Grant who grabbed me. It was Wilbur Downs. "We do this for Sam. You got that."

All I could do was nod. Then he dragged me back onto the field and placed me unceremoniously where I should be. It was a good thing, too, because I was kind of afraid that my legs were going to give out.

Second down. Two minutes to go. We were on their sixteen yard line. I bobbled the snap again but was able to get it off. The wide receiver snagged it and ran off the field for a short gain. The scoreboard said we had twelve yards to go.

Third down. Two more plays, and too much time to run out the clock. I glanced at Coach Grant, and he told me to "Go. Run the next play." I saw what he was doing. It was too risky to go for a field goal. Who knew what would happen in this mud. We'd already missed three. Our kicker was spooked, for sure. I wondered what would happen if Pip was given the chance to make the kick.

The ball snapped into my hands, and I handed it to our running back, who plowed through the line and got another three yards. It was fourth down, nine yards to go into the end zone. This was our last shot.

I glanced at the sideline to see if one of our kickers would join me. They didn't. Once again, Coach Grant gave me the signal to keep going. The best I could do was score a touchdown. The worst was get sacked, fumble the ball, and let Pinkerton College pick it up and run it down to the other end zone.

I tried to push that from my brain, but I felt like it was the first time I'd ever played football. I closed my eyes for half a second and breathed in slowly. "Let's go, Greco," said Wilbur Downs.

I called out the play, but it sounded wrong coming out of my mouth. Then I did something stupid. I didn't go by the playbook. I didn't hand the ball off to our running back so that we could get as close to the end zone as possible. Instead I dropped back and felt the collective gasp from the crowd.

I looked left. Nothing. Right. Nothing. Down the center, still nothing. Everyone was covered up or on the ground. Then two Pinkerton College players, big boys, broke through my line and zeroed in. I tried to juke right, but my foot slipped, and I almost ended up on the ground. I planted my left hand and got back to my feet; there was only one thing I could do. Put my head down and do exactly what I would do if I was still on the defensive line.

I plowed right through the first guy. I literally flung him over my head. I'm not sure how. It was instinct. Survival. How I kept the football? I have no idea, but with the second guy, my left hand went out, planted in his chest, and miraculously, he didn't keep coming. He slipped to the side. He was on the ground, and I was all by myself.

I heard nothing. I saw only the end zone. The rest was a blur. I slipped. I slid. I dodged tackles. If it were possible, I'd probably punched and kicked my way. I don't know if you call it grit and determination or an out-of-body experience. I'd say the latter. When I finally came to,

I was being hoisted in the air like a trophy by none other than Wilbur Downs.

That's when lightning did strike the stadium, and all the lights went out. A thunder boom rattled the ground, and whistles shrilled all around. Apparently, Pinkerton College had enough. The game was called. We won by seven points because we didn't have the time to kick an extra point. I'll never forget, there was exactly one minute and nine seconds left on the clock.

The thunderstorm lasted for three hours. We rinsed off with cold water in the dark, toweled off, slipped into clothes, and got back onto the bus. Coach Grant wasn't there. He'd gone to the hospital with Sam. Wilbur Downs sat by himself, face in his hands, the entire way home. All I could think about as my teammates clapped me on the back was what the hell happened?

Chapter 20

There were no celebratory parties that night. It was Downs who ordered us to go to our rooms and go to sleep. Tomorrow morning we'd see Sam.

At 9:00 a.m., there was a bus waiting. The entire football team boarded. Coach Grant was still absent. We drove the two hours back the way we'd come in silence, like we were going to a funeral. When we arrived at the hospital, the security staff said there were too many of us. Coach Grant appeared. He was wearing more than a five-o'clock shadow. He looked tired and grim.

"Downs and Greco with me," he said.

Downs gave me a look but didn't say anything. We followed Coach Grant to the elevators, and there was silence as we went up to the third floor. Coach Grant held me back when we got to Sam's room, and Downs walked in. As soon as he broke the threshold, I heard him sob. He was in there for a good ten minutes.

When he came back out, his eyes were puffy and red. Coach Grant patted him on the back and said to me, "It's your turn."

Propped up in the hospital bed, Sam's leg was up in one of those old slings. Nowadays, we'd probably do it differently, and he'd be up and walking already. But in 1989, it was basically still the Middle Ages. To my surprise, Sam looked good, minus a bruise on his cheek that did little to diminish his optimism.

"There's our hero," he said, shaking my hand and then patting the bed for me to sit down. "I heard what happened," he said. "Great work."

"Yeah." I didn't know what to say, but the words just tumbled out. "I really don't know what happened. I swear I blinked, and then I was in the end zone. Has that ever happened to you?"

"All the time," Sam said. "It's like we get in some kind of zone, some alternate reality. Our body takes over, and when we wake up, we're either splattered on the ground or standing with our hands up in the end zone. It's the funniest thing."

"Yeah," I agreed. "So, how's the leg?" Dumb question.

Sam's mouth dipped into a frown for the first time, but he recovered quickly. "It's not good, Greco. Coach hasn't told you."

"No, he hasn't told us anything."

Sam nodded as if that was what he expected. "I made the doctors tell me the truth, though my mom says she wants a second opinion. Probably even a third. I guess I'll go along with it, but I believe this doctor seems like a good guy. He used to be a Navy SEAL. Can you believe that?"

I nodded.

"So anyway, this SEAL doctor tells me, completely honest, that this is a career killer."

"You mean you'll never walk again?" I asked.

"No, not that, but my football days are over, Greco, just like that."

"You don't seem too upset," I said.

Sam shrugged. "Sure, I'm good enough to play for Jefferson State. I could probably get picked up after the draft, be a backup for a backup, that sort of thing. But I never came to Jefferson State to play football. Did you know that?"

I shook my head.

"When I was a sophomore, Coach suggested I do volunteer work. That volunteer work ended up with me coaching an inner-city school football team. Those kids were a hard nut to crack, but once I did . . . it's the best thing that ever happened to me, Greco, the best damn thing. You know those kids still write me letters? One kid was failing in school, and now he's getting straight As. I can't do that playing football, but

I can do that coaching. So, no, I'm not that sad. This just means that maybe I can do that faster."

I couldn't believe he was so calm about this. Who knew how much rehab he had in front of him? Who knew how this would affect his life? But he was already moving on to his real dream.

"Does that mean you're not on the team anymore?"

"Hell no," he said. "You can't get rid of me that easy. We've got a whole season ahead of us, and I don't care if you've got to push me in my wheelchair. I'm going to be on that sideline, and I'm going to tell you exactly what to do and what not to do. You hear me?"

He'd gone serious; all I could do was sit there and nod my head.

"But listen. About Downs. You can see he's taking this real hard. He thinks it's his fault, but it's not. I told him that. He'll figure it out in time. And he's a good man to have on your side, I promise."

I nodded. Mainly because I thought that's what Sam wanted.

A nurse entered the room with a tray of food and one of those little cups filled with pills. "It's time for your pain medication," she said.

"Please tell me there's a burger and fries on that tray," Sam said.

"Meatloaf and JELL-O," the nurse said proudly.

"You can give the meatloaf to him," Sam said, pointing at me. The nurse gave him the pill cup, and Sam took it dry.

"Send in Coach, will you?"

"Sure, no problem," I said, getting up from the bed and then walking to the door.

"And, hey, Greco?"

"Yeah, Sam."

"Chin up, okay?"

I raised my head and nodded at him, though I didn't feel like keeping my chin up. I wondered how this guy with a leg that was basically messed up beyond repair could say chin up, but I would eventually learn that there were many gifts in life that didn't require a one hundred percent healthy body. Sometimes, all it took was a little bit of faith.

Chapter 21

Coach wasn't with Sam long, and when he came downstairs, he only had a few words for us. I don't remember exactly what he said, probably something about getting back to work, thinking ahead of the season, all the obvious stuff. For some reason, I do remember he said, "All right, now let's get you all back home. I'm sure you have plenty of homework to do."

It was the first time I thought of homework since the day before, and I kicked myself for not bringing my books on the bus. Others had; Leroy had. Hell, he'd barely looked up from his textbooks on the way back to Pinkerton College. Unfortunately, we weren't in the same classes, or else I would've borrowed a book. I thought about the other players on the team, and unfortunately, the couple of players who did have classes with me had done the same as me—come empty handed— so I'd have to wait until we got back to school.

As we pulled away from the hospital, I thought about what Sam had said about sticking by Downs. Then I thought about every teammate that I needed to have on my side. It wasn't like a political campaign, but it was me proving myself to them. Sure, I'd had what people were calling the game's winning touchdown. Technically, we were still ahead by one, but my play had been sloppy, and I needed to figure out how to get my quarterback feet firm and planted, my arm strong and precise.

The bus dropped us off at the stadium. I made it a point to check in with the upperclassmen I knew would already be on with me. My center, for sure. He was protective no matter who was standing behind him. The wide receivers were eager to chat. They wanted to catch the ball. They wanted to score touchdowns. My running backs didn't say much. They tended to stick together, rough and tumble like their positions required.

Most of the team had cleared out. I turned around and looked for Leroy. Instead, I found a Mercedes convertible across the parking lot and a beautiful girl waving a tiny flag with Jefferson State University colors. It's not an exaggeration to say that something inside my chest fluttered. Somebody elbowed me in the side. I looked, and it was Leroy. "There's your girl, man. Talk to her."

"I know what to do," I said.

"You sure? Because I can write out a script if you want."

I was about to tell him where he could shove his script, but he ran away, giggling, and I walked toward Sheila, who was leaning against the hood of her beautiful car. "What are you doing here?" I asked, hoping my words didn't sound as stupid and nervous as they felt in my head.

"Just showing school spirit," she said, waving the little flag. Then she said, "Seriously, I heard about what happened to Sam. I'm sorry."

I nodded and sat next to her.

She nodded. "How do you feel?"

"I'm still processing."

"That's natural," she said. Then she sounded nervous. "I assume me showing up here messes up your plans."

"Plans?" I asked.

"Sure. Don't you have a celebration party to get to or something like that?"

I laughed. "I've got studying to get to. No time for parties." We both laughed nervously, and then I reached out and grabbed her hand. "It's good to see you," I said. "I didn't know if I'd see you again."

"What, you thought I'd use you up and throw you away?" she said, smiling.

"I didn't know what to think. I didn't want to assume."

She nodded, leaned toward me, and kissed me on the cheek. "I've got studying to do too. How about I drive you to your room, you get your books, and you come to my place? We'll study together." If I had allowed myself, I would've jumped onto the hood and screamed *Yes* at the top of my lungs. But instead, I think what I did was nod and say "Okay, that sounds good."

We passed Leroy on the way, and as payback for his teasing, I gave him the flying middle finger. I rushed up to our room, stuffed a bunch of books into my backpack, and ran back to her car. By then, Leroy was there talking to Sheila. "It was good to meet you, Sheila," he said, pushing off the car. Then he gave me a wink and a wave. I slipped into the car, and Sheila peeled away from the curb. "I like your roommate," she said.

"Yeah, he's okay."

"Okay?" she asked.

"He's better than okay. I think he's my best friend."

She reached across and grabbed my hand and gave it a squeeze. "I hope we can be friends, too, Greco. I really do." I nodded because what I wanted to say was *I want us to be more than friends,* but of course I didn't have the balls.

Chapter 22

"Let's work in the kitchen," Sheila said when we pulled into the garage. "Are you hungry?"

"Does a leopard have spots?" I asked.

She rolled her eyes and said, "You need to work on your jokes."

"Fine. You make lunch, and I'll work on my jokes."

She slapped me playfully on the arm. "You get to work. I'll make lunch. We'll work on jokes later. I've got a library full of them."

I sat on a barstool at the big island in her kitchen. I tried to work, but instead, I found my eyes flickering over to Sheila. I was sure I'd never seen anything sexier than this woman making sandwiches. She set the plate before me and asked if I wanted chips.

"Sure. What do you have?"

"Anything you want. Potato chips, Doritos . . ."

"Doritos, please," I said.

I pushed the books away, and we dug into lunch. Like before, I finished before Shelia had three bites of her own. Then she pushed her plate toward me, and I asked, "Are you sure?" She nodded. She seemed to get a kick out of me eating so much, and yes, I ate everything.

"Coffee or tea?" she asked, getting up from her chair.

"Coffee with a lot of sugar, please," I said.

She made a face like it was the most disgusting thing in the world.

"What? I'm a new coffee drinker," I said.

Back home, caffeine was a premium, something I couldn't afford. When I'd stayed up late studying in high school, I had pure Coca-Cola that I bought at school because it was cheaper. I'd buy six cans at a time and shove them into my backpack. I dug into my ancient Chinese history textbook while Sheila made coffee. When it was done, she brought a cup over along with a jar of sugar.

"You can put your sugar in. I can't. That's sacrilege."

"Hey, the Italians put plenty of sugar in their coffee."

"I'm not Italian," she said in a fake haughty accent. "I'm from Manhattan."

"Manhattan," I said, standing up and then grabbing her around the waist. "What else do you guys do in Manhattan?"

"We study," she said, touching the tip of my nose with her index finger. "Now, get back to work. If you're good, we can have dessert later."

It took every ounce of willpower I had to focus on work, but since she had pulled out her books, too, and seemed not nearly as distracted as me, I did get some studying done. I'd say now, it was probably more hormones than anything. Maybe it was the teenager in me still thinking if I didn't do my work and she tested me, she would make me go home. Stupid, I know, but I was eighteen. Remember?

"What time do you have class tomorrow?" she asked.

"Nine," I said.

We'd been a couple of hours into our studies by then. I was finally getting in the groove. Shelia had finished whatever she was working on and was reading a book, some old novel I didn't recognize.

"What about you?"

"I don't have class tomorrow," she said. "One of the perks of being a grad student."

"Wait, you don't have class tomorrow?"

"Nope. I only have classes Tuesdays and Thursdays. On Wednesdays, I'm a teacher's assistant, but the rest of the week is mine."

"How do I get that?"

"Become a grad student," Sheila said. "Now, get back to work. I'm thinking about what I'm going to make for dinner."

My stomach grumbled at that. The next time I looked at the clock, it was 5:00 p.m., and my eyes were starting to go blurry.

"I need a break," I said. "Do you mind if I take a walk outside?"

Sheila looked up from her book. "If that's what you think you need."

I didn't know what she meant with her comment until she put her book down and looked at me—like really looked at me. Then I understood.

"Oh," I said.

"Oh." She sat back, grinning.

I took her hand and walked her to the bedroom. It would be some time before we ate dinner.

◆　◆　◆

"I feel like beer," Sheila said while we were lying in bed after early dessert.

"You don't look like a beer," I said.

"Ha ha, very funny. I told you, later we'll work on your sense of humor. Right now, you get to fetch."

Instead of fetching, I rolled over on top of her.

"Uh-uh," she said. "You owe me a beer. Now fetch, starting quarterback, or I might not let you spend the night."

That's all I needed to hear. I slipped on my boxers and sprinted from the room. When I hit the hallway, I walked and thought about the kind of life this could be. A beautiful house, a beautiful girl. Is this what my future looked like? When I walked into the kitchen and headed for the fridge, I didn't notice the figure in the living room.

"Look, honey, Sheila has a visitor."

Oh shit, I thought, and tried to hide behind the kitchen island.

"Leave the poor boy alone, dear," a male voice said.

"I'm sorry, but I . . ." I blabbered something. I don't remember what it was. A tall man with graying hair who looked like he would've been very much at home at the helm of a yacht strolled into the kitchen.

"I'm David Sinclair, Sheila's father, and you are?"

"Greco, sir. I mean, Michael Greco."

He stuck out his hand, and I shook it. "Nice to meet you, Mr. Greco. This is my wife, Claudia."

She waved with her fingers, and I noticed she was sipping on a flute of what looked like champagne.

"Why don't you return to what you were fetching, Mr. Greco? My wife and I can wait."

"Sure," I said, but, half-naked as I was, I didn't feel like going to the fridge and fetching the two beers. So instead, as nonchalantly as possible, I strolled back to Sheila's room.

"Hey," I whispered. "Your parents are here."

She sat up in bed, the sheet wrapped around her body. "Did you get to meet them?" She wasn't surprised, and that surprised me.

"They saw me like this."

"And?"

"Should I leave? I can go out the window."

"Don't be silly. And hey, where's my beer?"

What I wanted to say was *How can you think of beer at a time like this?* We'd got caught naked red handed. Instead, I said, "I forgot."

To my amazement, she stood up with the sheet still wrapped around her and didn't put clothes on. She did not slip into a robe. She grabbed my hand and dragged me out of the room. We walked back to the kitchen with me looking sheepish and wholly embarrassed. We went through the kitchen and into the living room.

"Hello, Mom."

"Dear," Claudia said.

Mr. Sinclair stood up, and Sheila let go of my hand and gave him a hug.

"How are you, honey?"

"I'm great, Dad. Did you meet Greco?"

"You call him Greco?" Mr. Sinclair said.

"Everybody does and you should too." She looked at me. "Right?"

I nodded. This was one of the weirdest interactions I'd ever had in my life.

"It's good to meet you again, Greco," he said, shaking my hand for the second time that day.

"It's good to meet you, too, sir."

He did not tell me to call him David.

"Since you two surprised us, I don't mean to be rude, but we were about to have a beer. See you in, say, thirty minutes?"

"It's a deal," Mr. Sinclair said.

"Fine by me," Claudia Sinclair said.

We returned to the kitchen, where Sheila grabbed two beers from the fridge, and then we went back to her room.

"Hey, I really think I should leave," I said.

"Oh, you're not leaving now."

"I'm not?"

"No. Here, drink your beer."

"Look, I don't feel comfortable here with your parents."

"What's wrong with my parents?" Sheila asked.

"Nothing. It's just . . ."

"What? Have you never met your girlfriend's parents before?"

The look on my face must have said it all.

"Wait, you've never met a girlfriend's parents?"

"Didn't I tell you? I never really dated."

She looked at me sincerely and put her hand on my cheek.

"Greco, what am I going to do with you?"

And then she pulled me to the bed, and the beers were forgotten.

Chapter 23

We emerged from the room exactly thirty minutes later, showered and dressed. Sheila went straight to her parents and gave them each a big hug. I could tell by the gesture that they were close, and though both Mother and Father Sinclair looked like they could be on the cover of a hoity-toity magazine, they were kind, and with me, they were gentle.

"I had an idea," Claudia said.

"Great. Mom and her exciting ideas," Sheila said, her arm wrapped around her father. "Do tell, Mother."

"We should go into the city and have dinner."

"I was going to make dinner here, Mom."

"Forget about that. I want to spend time with you. With you and your new friend."

"He's my boyfriend," Sheila said. I didn't know if we'd ever discussed that, but why the hell was I going to say I wasn't her boyfriend?

"Fine, then. Would you and your boyfriend—"

"His name is Greco, Mom."

"Do I have to call him that?"

I was about to tell her that, no, she didn't. She could call me anything she wanted. Before I could, she continued.

"Fine, then. Would you and Greco like to come to dinner with your father and me in the city?"

"Mom, I don't know. Greco's got class tomorrow and—"

"Hey, it's okay with me," I said. Screw it, right? In for a penny . . . besides, something about the relationship between them captivated me. I'd never had this. They seemed genuinely interested and loving with each other. I wanted to soak in it if only for one night. Hell, I'd even be on my best behavior.

"Fine. That settles it," Claudia said. "Greco, do you have anything else you can wear?"

"I've got some clothes back in my room." I was wearing what I wore on the team bus earlier in the day, which was the team jumpsuit.

"David, I'm sure you have something he can borrow here."

"Of course," Mr. Sinclair said. "Greco, come with me." He let go of his daughter and ushered me from the room. Mother and daughter instantly paired up and were whispering when we left. "What size suit do you wear, Greco? Your inseam?"

"I'm sorry. I don't know," I said.

"That's okay. You're broader than I am in the chest, but I'm a little taller, so I'm sure there's something we can make work."

I thought maybe there was a cardboard box with some old clothes that he would let me rummage through, but nope. There was a full walk-in closet with suits and what I would come to know as resort wear, expensive from head to toe. "Sir, I can't wear these clothes."

"Why not? You don't think you'll fit?"

"I—"

"It's fine, really. I rarely wear this stuff anyway. Claudia makes me keep it here. Here, try this on." He pulled out a sport coat, some slacks, and a button-down shirt. "What size shoe do you wear?"

I told him. "Perfect. We're the same size." He gave me a pair of loafers and shooed me to the bathroom. Sure, the jacket was a little tight. My arms and chest were bigger than his, but the pants fit fine, and my fat fingers were able to button the shirt. I walked out, and Mr. Sinclair said, "Perfect. Now why don't you join the ladies, and I'll get dressed. I'll meet you out there in a couple of minutes."

When I returned to the living room, Sheila was gone, but Claudia was pouring herself another glass of champagne. "Greco. You look perfect." She walked over and smoothed the lapels of the coat. "You're a bit more fit than my husband; don't tell him I said so. Men are so self-conscious about that sort of thing. But, my, do you dress up well. Now, come sit down. I think we have at least five minutes. I want to hear everything about you."

It turned out that the city was New York City, not Chicago, which was forty-five minutes away. The chauffeur pulled up to Sheila's house in a stretch limo. I had never been in a limo. Then the driver took us to a private airport, where we boarded a private plane. On board the plane was a personal staff. There was more champagne, which I needed by that point, and hors d'oeuvres, and Mr. Sinclair asked if I wanted to watch the pilots take off.

"No," I said, "I much prefer to be sitting and buckled in." I'd only been on a handful of flights in my life, never private. While this should have been a treat, I was, in effect, terrified. Fearful I would do something wrong, like spill champagne all over Sheila's mom and dad. Afraid that this private plane would crash, and I would never get to see Tommy again. Scared I was going to say something stupid and screw up this whole beautiful thing.

But if Sheila noticed my unease, she didn't show it. In fact, she looked amazing. She wore a simple navy blue dress. I remember the necklace she was wearing was a pendant with a star. She'd done up her hair so that it was piled on top of her head so you could see her neck. As I sipped my champagne, I thought she was, without a doubt, the most beautiful woman I'd ever seen.

I won't go into all the details of what happened when we got to the city. There was another private limo and then a restaurant that looked like a hole in the wall, but when you went inside, it was a small place with only three tables, and the owner knew the Sinclairs personally. He hugged everyone, asking Sheila how school was going. Then they brought out food without anyone having ordered. It was delicious, and

Claudia got a good laugh from how much I ate. I'd had enough champagne and wine by that point that I really didn't care. I was starting to enjoy myself. If this was what life could be, I wanted more of it. This evening would plant the seeds of success deep within me that I would carry for years to come.

But it was the humility and the love shown between parents and daughter that captivated me. Later, when I would have my own boys, I would remember that love; I would remember the Sinclairs' generosity. For now, let's relish the memory that I was flown to New York City in a private jet and enjoyed what was possibly the best meal of my life with a beautiful girl and her kind parents, and each step along the way, something inside me grew. Whether it was hope, or a new vision for my life, I didn't know at the time.

But little did I know that as soon as I got back to school, my cruel world would once again come crashing down, and that night in New York City would be forgotten.

Chapter 24

The next weeks were tough but exhilarating. I somehow kept up with everything: my schoolwork, learning how to be starting quarterback, trying to earn the respect of my team. Then there was dating Sheila and going along with whatever adventures Leroy, and now Pip, concocted.

It turned out that Pip was a world-class prankster. Everything from shaving cream in your locker to tying shoelaces to a desk was in his repertoire. He got away with it because he didn't look like a prankster. He looked like someone pulled out of a country-club polo roster.

We kept winning games. At first, it was by a field goal, then by a touchdown. By October, we were beginning to hit our stride. Leroy was starting to rack up tackles and had two interceptions and two fumble recoveries to his name. Coach Grant was bringing Pip on for the long field goal attempts, ones that our starting kicker couldn't hit. Once, Pip missed a sixty-yard field goal by mere inches. We were all excelling.

The other great thing was my two new best friends worked as hard as I did. We pushed each other to be better. When everybody else went home after practice, we stayed and kept running drills. Leroy still dreamed of being a running back, so he played off the line, and Pip would stand in as wide receiver. The three of us were inseparable. I wanted to spend more time with Sheila, but she insisted that I enjoy my first year at school. And I did. Though, I admit that when I was hanging out with my friends, I was also thinking about her.

How could I not? Meeting her family and the trip to New York had planted something deep within me. Even though they dressed like they'd been born on Savile Row, they were kind and humble. Now, Claudia was unafraid to tell the maître d' that they wanted their usual table and that "No, the table next to it would not do." These people knew what they wanted, and Sheila was no exception. Sometimes she would call me at one in the morning, and I would hurry right over.

I'd taken to driving when we were together because, honestly, I didn't trust her. She liked to go too fast. I came to recognize that there was something else driving her, some need to move at blinding speed. She was a bit like my friends; she was trying to squeeze every moment out of the day.

We would walk by a field of flowers, and she would insist that we go sit in the middle of them and simply enjoy a few minutes. Of course I went along. When I think back, those are some of my fondest memories.

But like all memories, at that point in my life, there were still shadows waiting on the sidelines. Some days there were no faxes, and others there were three or four. I would decipher them with my father's Bible, take care of them the best I could, but I knew I could only do so much from a distance. Soon enough, I would need to go home and negotiate face to face.

It was still early in the season, but we had a bye coming up. I told Sheila I needed to go home, and I asked my friends to cover for me.

Luckily, my Friday classes let out early. I bought a bus ticket, said goodbye to Sheila, and headed for home. I tried to study the whole way, but my gut twisted in knots.

Do you see a common pattern? I'm older now, but still, my stomach twists. It's probably something genetic—the anxiety deep within me, most likely handed down by generations of Greco men.

I shouldn't have been surprised when I got home and found Mom stumbling around the kitchen. I made a point of slamming the door so she would get the hint that I was there. She whirled around, teetering, but she held onto the kitchen counter and said, "Oh God, my baby boy."

I walked to her and hugged her, smelling the booze and the fact that she hadn't showered. "Hi, Mom," I said. She tried to kiss me on the cheek, but I stepped away.

"Now, why do you have to be like that?" she asked.

I didn't want to get into it. I didn't want to say *Stay away from me, Mom. You stink.* But the fact was, I didn't want to be home.

"How's Tommy?" I asked instead.

"He's at school. You know him. Never makes his bed, doesn't make the breakfast that you used to. Pours me a bowl of cereal and says he's doing a good job."

I wanted to tell her that she could get her own breakfast, that she was an adult, and Tommy was a kid. Again, I kept my mouth shut.

"What time does he get home?"

Though I knew the answer, I wanted to see if she knew. How bad had she gotten?

"Four o'clock on a regular day, but six o'clock when he has practice."

Tommy played football, too, though he wasn't as good as me. I'd made my old coach promise he'd keep an eye on him.

The best way to keep him away from home and away from Mom's influence was to keep him busy. Maybe I'd stop out at the high school and see how he was doing. Check in with Coach, and see if Tommy was working hard or slacking off, probably the latter.

I was about to tell Mom that I was going to walk to the school, but someone else came in and said, "Well, look what the cat dragged in."

It was my uncle Freddy. If it was possible, his beer gut had gotten even bigger. And when he walked into the kitchen, he didn't come over and shake my hand. He went straight for Mom, put an arm around her waist, and kissed her wetly on the lips. When he saw the look on my mom's face, he looked at me and her and, pretending that he was being sheepish, said, "Oops, did I ruin the surprise?"

Chapter 25

I don't know how I didn't beat my uncle Freddy to a pulp right then and there. Maybe I should have. Maybe it would've fixed some of the problems coming down the road, but I didn't. I tried to act nonchalant, like it didn't matter. But it did matter. The bastard was in my house and probably sleeping with my mom. Why hadn't Tommy told me? He and I were going to have words.

"I'm going to the high school," I said, heading for the door.

"Okay, honey," Mom said, trying to sound sweet but slurring her words. "I'll have dinner ready for you when you get back."

I was going to tell her not to bother, but if I had opened my mouth again, I would've said many things that I'd regret.

"And Greco," Uncle Freddy chimed in, "let me know if you need any help with your chores." He put special emphasis on "chores." He knew why I was in town. I wondered how much he knew about my fax messages.

Instead of engaging, I ignored him and walked out the door. I wasn't dressed for it, but I ran all the way to the high school. It was two miles, which wasn't far, but by the time I got there, I was lathered in sweat. My jeans were sticking to my legs, and I felt sick. I followed the sound of whistles and shouts to the football field, and when I approached, my old coach turned and smiled wide.

"Well, well, if it ain't Greco the Great!" That's what he used to call me because there was a time when I had a huge chip on my shoulder. Coach had worked it out of me, and now it was just a joke between two men. He shook my hand and then pulled me into a bear hug. "It's good to see you, Greco."

"You, too, Coach."

"Aw, come on. You can call me by my first name now. You're a college boy."

"I think that's a bridge too far, Coach."

"Fine. Fine. Have it your way. What are you doing back home? I thought you'd be busy getting ready for next week."

"You've been following the games?"

Coach nodded. "If I had known you'd have that kind of arm, hell, I could have gotten you a scholarship to Florida State."

I didn't want to go down that rabbit hole, so I said, "How's Tommy doing?"

His smile turned to a frown. "The Greco boys were not made the same," he said. "You worked your tail off. Tommy chases tail. Look at him right now."

I looked across the field and saw Tommy goofing around on the sideline. He hadn't noticed that I was there.

"You want me to talk to him?" I asked.

"I can handle it."

I was still going to talk with Tommy. My high school coach was more uncle than my uncle Freddy. Hell, he'd filled in as father more times than I could recall. Once, he'd let me crash in his office on a four-night stretch when things were bad at home.

Coach snapped his fingers. "Hey, I have an idea."

"Coach, you know I never like it when you say that."

He was grinning ear to ear. "You'll like this one. How's your voice?"

"My voice?"

"Yeah," he said, nodding.

"It feels okay, I guess."

Without warning, he blew his whistle long and hard. Then he looked at me, winked, and said, "How would you like to scare a bunch of high school kids, Greco?"

That got me grinning. "Sounds good to me, Coach."

When practice was over, the entire high school football team was wobbling on their legs. Coach had let me put them through drills, ones I'd done back when I was playing on the same field and ones I'd learned at college. I was like a recruit who got to come back as a drill instructor. I'm no sadist, but come on. I wasn't even twenty years old, and I got to be the coach for the day. Coach's long whistle signaled the end of practice, and everyone gathered around.

"Take a knee," he bellowed. Everyone got down to one knee, although some slumped down onto their rears. "I said, take a knee," Coach said. Tommy had been one of the few to fall onto his butt. We hadn't said two words to each other. I'd worked him the hardest. "Boys, how about we give Greco here a proper hurrah? Ready? Hurrah, on three. One, two, three."

"Hurrah!" the team echoed.

"Now, Mr. Greco, who, as you know, is now the starting quarterback for Jefferson State University, will give us all a little lesson on what hard work means."

"Hey, I thought he already did that, Coach," someone said in the crowd. Others chuckled.

"Pipe down," Coach said, but he wasn't angry. There was a little grin on his lips. "What I mean is, Greco is going to tell you what hard work gets you. What dedication, determination, what all those words mean in the real world." He slapped me on the back. "Go ahead, Greco. The floor is all yours."

He hadn't prepared me for this, but whether it was the way these boys looked at me—sweat on their brows, grass stains on their pants—or the fact that Tommy was in the crowd, and in fact, paying attention, the words came.

I began with "Everything you think you know is wrong. Let me tell you what happens when life punches you in the face."

Chapter 26

The coach thanked me for my words and dismissed the team. I told Tommy I'd meet him back home. I had an errand to run, and I literally ran into town, making sure I wasn't followed. Maybe I was being paranoid. I couldn't be too careful. My destination wasn't far.

I went straight for the bank, which would close in ten minutes. The familiar face of Mrs. Mockingham greeted me. I'd known her my entire life. She taught Sunday school and worked as a teller at the bank.

"You come here and give me a hug," she said, but then she saw that I was covered in sweat. "Greco, where have you been? I thought you were a put-together college boy now."

"Sorry, Mrs. Mockingham, I was helping out at the high school."

She smiled at that. "I'll bet those boys and the coach were happy to see you."

"Yes, ma'am. They were."

"I take it you didn't come by to say hello."

"No, ma'am, I hoped to get into my box."

I found out about the safe-deposit box after my father died. I was the only one who knew it existed. Mrs. Mockingham glanced at the clock on the wall.

"I've got bridge at the church, but"—she paused, thinking—"how much time do you need?"

"Not long, I promise," I said.

"Okay, I'll have them open it up for you."

I'd been through the process twice before, but as with the previous times, when I was escorted back to the private room to open my father's safe-deposit box, I felt like a spy. When the door of the secure room closed, I opened the box, and it revealed the only contents, a well-worn journal.

The journal held a record of every transaction my father had made in his adult life, including ongoing business relationships. There were other, more sordid details of certain "friends" included, spelled out in Dad's unique phrasing. These special bits could only be used for one thing: blackmail. The notes were meticulous and neat. They went back to before I was born. It was bequeathed to me in private by an attorney I had never met until my father's death. His instructions had been quite clear. I was the only one to have access to the contents of the bank box. The lawyer didn't know what it contained. He only knew about the safe-deposit box, and he was the one who set it up with the bank so I would have access to it. The first thing I'd found in the box all those months ago was a simple note from Dad. It read, "Greco, I won't try to explain everything I did. I hope one day you'll understand that I lived the best I could. Hopefully this'll be good insurance, one last gift from your pops. Don't let anyone see it. Keep it safe." The note was taped to the journal. I sat staring at said journal now. I'd burned the note after reading it on that first visit. I debated taking the ledger with me but decided not to. It was too valuable and held too many secrets. Dad was right. It was my insurance policy.

I pulled the piece of paper with the notes from the outstanding faxes out of my pocket. It wasn't hard to find the log entries in my father's handwriting. A favor given here; a debt owed there. All told, there were nine items, and in under fifteen minutes, I was able to jot down the details I needed. Then I put the journal back in the safe-deposit box and knocked for the man who'd let me out of the room.

"Did you get everything you needed?" Mrs. Mockingham asked when I went back into the lobby.

"Yes, ma'am. Thank you."

"How long are you in town, Greco? Are you coming to church on Sunday?"

"I'm not sure, Mrs. Mockingham. I might have to leave tomorrow."

"I understand. I heard that you're playing quarterback now. We're all very proud of you."

"Thank you," I said, my face coloring.

"Please give my best to your family."

"I will. Thanks again."

I left the bank thinking I'd take a stroll through town. Maybe I'd bump into some of my old friends, but honestly, that's the last thing I wanted. Not today. Maybe I'd get a bite to eat. Who knew what Mom was whipping up? I'd probably have to order pizza for the family and, God forbid, for Uncle Freddy.

But I hadn't even turned the corner when a car honked, and I looked over and saw Uncle Freddy's copper-toned Buick parked on the side of the road. Uncle Freddy waved me over, and I debated ignoring him and walking on, but that would probably get me and my family in more trouble than I wanted. I walked over and avoided the plume of smoke he blew out the window.

"I hear you stopped by the high school," he said.

"I told you that's where I was going," I said.

"Feel good to be the big man on campus?"

I didn't answer. He took a long suck from his cigar, held it in, then blew it out. "How was your visit to the bank?"

How did he know that I'd gone to the bank? Then I remembered that Uncle Freddy knew everyone in town. Who had called him? Was it Mrs. Mockingham? Was it the guy that had let me into the private room? It didn't matter. I'd have to be more careful.

"I'm going home," I said.

"Okay, but don't you forget, I'm taking care of your family now."

I turned around. "You stay away from my family," I snapped.

He didn't look shocked; in fact, he laughed. "Why don't you tell your mother? She's not complaining." He licked his lips, and I thought about putting my fist through his face.

He glanced down at my clenched hands. "They teach you to fight in school? I seem to remember you're a pansy when it comes to fighting." He opened the car door and stepped out. He set his cigar on top of the car and cracked his knuckles. "Come on then," he said. "You want to fight? I'll teach you to fight."

I'd seen Uncle Freddy fight. Though I thought I could take him, I also knew that despite his languid outward appearance, when he got his blood rising, he was like a rhino. I saw him bash the heads of two young punks like they were cantaloupes. One was in a wheelchair for life, and the other one had been in a coma for six weeks.

"I'm going home," I said again.

He nodded. "Good choice. I'll see you around, nephew."

I turned and walked home. What I should have done was walk straight to the bus stop and head back to school, but there were things to be done. Loose ends to tie up. But I wondered whether Uncle Freddy would follow me at every turn.

Chapter 27

I'm not sure how I made it through that night and the next day. As Saturday evening rolled around, I was exhausted, morally spent, and eager to go back to school.

Mom begged me to stay for another night. She said she wanted to show me off to everybody at church. I couldn't believe she still went to church. I wondered if she went to church drunk. Tommy mostly avoided me, and maybe that was for the best. I didn't have time to clean up his mess. I was still trying to clean up my father's.

In every meeting I took that Saturday, every lowlife and long-lost cousin accepted me with feigned respect as if I were my father's heir. That was the last thing I wanted. They were all liars and cheats. I had the paperwork to prove it.

Now, one thing I want to make clear is I wasn't handing out wads of cash. We didn't have wads of cash. It was basically delivering the names of contacts, signing over rights, and transferring shell business accounts. That's where Dad's ledger came in. Without it, I was screwed. But once word got out—and it was out—I knew there would be many more favors. This ledger told the story of how many fly-by-night schemes my dad had been a part of. I didn't want to think about how many transactions were left. Here's a taste of what Dad was into: a minority ownership in a liquor shop–slot machine operation. A guarantee for commercial zoning of an outlet in downtown Chicago. The names of two trainers who could "fix" dogs down at the racetrack. Yeah, Dad was the original cornucopia of underworld entrepreneurs. The funny thing was, according to Dad's ledger, which I took at face value, we were the ones owed money and favors, not the other way around. The problem was, these were all handshake–smoke room deals, and I wasn't about to stick around for anything extra. I wanted to be done with all of it, and if that meant giving away what was meant as an inheritance, so be it. So I pressed just enough to get out clean. But the pressing was exhausting, though it honed my subtle negotiating skills for years to come.

When Saturday night rolled around, I went to the bus stop and was lucky enough to get the last ticket back to my true home, my new home. Leroy was gone when I got back to the dorm, and I crashed onto my bed. I didn't want to look at the fax because I knew there would be more encoded messages, love letters from the grave.

It was Sunday morning when I woke. Leroy was snoring in bed. Before I went to the bathroom, I saw there was, indeed, a pile of faxes. I took a long, hot shower, needing to burn and sanitize myself after my ordeal. But no amount of scrubbing could get rid of the feeling of grime, and I felt I was slowly being pulled into my father's web. He'd been subtle over the years. He was always saying I should make a big name for myself in sports and get a college education. But like my dreams showed, he was always educating me, always showing me the angles. For my part, I understood every single one. I was an apt pupil. Looking back now, I know that saved me. It saved my family. Because if that laundry list of problems had been given to Tommy, well, let's say I don't want to think about that.

After a shower, I went down to the dorm lounge to use the phone. I knew Sheila would be up. She was an early riser.

"Hello," she answered.

"Hey, it's me." I don't know what I expected, but maybe something more than what came next.

"Hi, Greco. I'm sorry. I'm busy right now. Can you call me back later?"

"Sure," I said. Before I could say anything else, she hung up.

I tried to put it out of my mind, but I wanted nothing more than to go to her place and be with somebody normal. Instead, I got dressed and went to work. I tried to call Sheila two more times that day. She never picked up. I thought about taking a bus to her place or maybe walking. It was a long walk, but I could make it. But I figured if she wanted to call me, she would call me.

At bedtime, you know those little worries that creep in? They start with something small, like somebody says something or looks at you funny, and then you're not in the right mood. Then you take a little comment and twist it the wrong way. My mangled brain was good at twisting, and did it do some spinning.

When I fell asleep, I dreamed that Sheila was with somebody else. I envisioned her with some faceless boy wonder on a private plane flying to Paris. But the image that woke me from a screaming sweat was the face of my father.

I sat up in bed and looked over at Leroy, who was looking at me.

"You okay?" he asked.

"Yeah. Sorry. Want me to go down to the lounge?"

"No, that's okay." I'm pretty sure Leroy sat up watching me as I went back to sleep.

I couldn't have asked for a better roommate or better friend. But that week, no number of friends could have saved me from myself. I didn't talk to Sheila on Monday. And though I thought I'd prepared for my quiz in statistics, I still failed. Then at practice, I couldn't get in a good rhythm. Coach made me do so many sprints that I swore I was going to vomit up my stomach.

When I tried to call Sheila that night, there was still no answer.

Screw her, I thought.

I slammed the phone down, and Leroy looked up from his studies.

"Everything okay?" he asked, the worry plain on his face.

"Fine," I said, slamming the receiver one more time for good measure.

"You sure? Because you don't look fine. And that phone can't take much more abuse."

"I said I'm fine," I barked.

He turned his head slowly back to his work. Then he looked back to me and said, "You know, Greco, you don't have to do it all on your own. I'm here. But I've had about enough of the attitude. Feel me?"

"Yeah, sorry," I said in a half-hearted attempt to get him to leave me alone.

From there, the week kept getting worse. I couldn't focus. The faxes kept coming in. I kept sneaking away to make secret calls, but the to-do list kept growing. Worst of all, Sheila never called me back. Leroy kept giving me looks. We barely talked.

And then to cap it all off, on Saturday, in view of our entire student body, I collapsed on the field. I couldn't make a handoff. I couldn't make a pass. Hell, I couldn't remember the plays. We got walloped by four touchdowns.

When we went to the locker room at the end of the game, all eyes were me. The only thing that Coach Grant said was "We can all do better. Remember that."

I didn't feel like I could do better. It felt like everything was getting worse. Screw football. Screw school. Maybe I should run away, take a bus down to Mexico, and disappear forever.

But what kept me from following that train of thought was waiting for me outside my dorm as I dragged myself home. Sitting on the steps, his lip cut, his face bruised, was my little brother, Tommy.

Chapter 28

I pulled my little brother inside and rushed him to my room. When the door was closed, I grabbed him by both sides of the face. He winced.

"What happened?" I asked. He wormed away from my grasp.

"Nothing, okay? I'm fine."

"Really? Because you sure don't look fine. And how the hell did you get here, anyway?"

"I hitchhiked," he said.

"You hitchhiked? You're fifteen."

"Yeah, dummy. That's why I hitchhiked, because I can't drive."

I exhaled. With Tommy, talking took finesse. He had a way of getting under my skin that made me boil. Right now, after the terrible loss on the football field and the week I'd had, I knew I was very close to my tipping point.

"Was it Uncle Freddy?" I asked. He laughed.

"No. Wasn't that fat fuck. Just some guys in the neighborhood."

"What guys?" I asked, already picking the usual suspects from my brain.

"Some guys that said they knew Dad."

"Why the hell did they do that to you?"

"I may have said some things," he said.

"What kind of things?"

"I don't know. Stuff like no one was ever as good as my dad. Stuff like that."

"Then they beat you up."

"Hey, I held my own, okay? I knocked out one dude's front teeth." He held up the fist, and I saw his bloody knuckles. That's when I noticed how much he'd grown. His shoulders were broader now, filling out his T-shirt. How had I missed it?

"What else did they say?" I asked.

"I don't know. Something about you getting your shit together; I didn't understand. What were they talking about, Mikey?"

Tommy didn't know about Dad's business dealings and didn't need to know. It was my business now. Tommy still held Dad high on a pedestal, and I was fine leaving it that way. But that led to the fight, to Tommy's words, which were always poorly picked, and now things could get dangerous.

"Listen to me. I'll call Mom, and I'll tell her that we planned this visit. I'll call your school too. I'll let your coach know, and he'll take care of everything with your teachers. You can stay for the night, but tomorrow I'm putting you on a bus back home. Do you understand?"

"Come on, man. I wanna stay. You know how many hot girls I've seen? One of them said she'd give me her number."

That I seriously doubted. Tommy still looked fifteen, and with his beat-up face, I don't think any college girl would've given him the time of day. But that was Tommy, always mouthing off, always talking a little too tall.

"You stay in this room; I'll order some pizza. I assume you haven't eaten." He shook his head. I would've been ashamed, but he didn't care. We were polar opposites, especially when responsibility was involved. I took it naturally; he brushed it off like a disease. The last thing I wanted was for him to sniff out what I'd been doing. Because with Tommy, you never knew when he'd run off at the mouth. What if he said something to our uncle Freddy? What if he said something to some more "friendly" neighbors? Worst of all, what if he said something to Mom, because she didn't know either? Mom was a big hot mess that needed to fix herself. There was nothing I could do about that, so I asked the only thing that made sense at that moment. "Do you want cheese or pepperoni pizza?"

Chapter 29

The next morning I got up before dawn. Leroy was snoring, and Tommy was curled up in a ball on the floor, half-covered in a blanket we'd scrounged from a girl two floors up. I left Tommy a note, though I figured I'd return before he woke. "Stay here. I'll bring food."

I slipped into my running shoes and took off down the road. When I got to the football offices, my coach's light was on. I knocked on his door, and he said, "Come in."

I walked into the room. The office walls were covered with pictures of every team he'd ever coached. Coach Grant wasn't married. He had no kids. We were his kids.

"Greco, a little early for you, isn't it?"

"Sorry, Coach. Were you in the middle of something?"

"No. Why don't you have a seat? Tell me what's on your mind."

I took a seat, and the words poured out without prompting. "Coach, about the game. I want to say I'm sorry and I'm going to work hard to—"

To that, he put up a hand. "While I appreciate the apology, I know you've already beat yourself up more than I ever could. Let's put the game and last week in the past."

"Yes, Coach," I said. I figured he wouldn't rake me over the coals, but I was relieved, nonetheless.

"How are things, Greco? School, family. You went home, didn't you?"

"Yes, sir."

"And?"

I told him some of the truth. "My mom's kind of a wreck, and my little brother, well, he's on his way to becoming a mess."

Coach Grant nodded. "Did I ever tell you that I lost my father when I was young? I was twelve. I have seven younger siblings, if you can believe that—Irish Catholic family. My mother came from poor immigrant stock. She was barely literate. My dad had been the bread-winner. When he died, the responsibility fell on me."

I didn't know that story. I wondered how many people he had told it to.

"That must have been hard, Coach."

Coach Grant nodded. "It was tough, but for most of my siblings, it brought us closer together. Those of us who are still around are very close, and I'm proud to say that I kept my end of the bargain, though there were days that, frankly, I wanted to quit. Do you understand that feeling, Greco?"

"Yes, sir, I do."

"Do you know what it's like to go hungry, Greco?"

"Yes, Coach."

"How many times have you gone hungry?"

"I'm not sure, Coach. A few."

"I went without food for exactly one hundred and seventeen meals. Not all in a row, of course. But if it was a choice between buying for-mula for my baby sister or getting lunch for my five-year-old brother, what do you think I was going to choose?"

"You were going to choose them."

"That's right, Greco. And ask me if I regret it."

"Do you regret it?"

"Not a single bit. Now ask me why."

"Why don't you regret it, Coach?"

"Because I can't change it, and because I did my best. I didn't always do everything well, but I was still a kid. Sure, there were days when I wanted to quit and run away and shirk my responsibility. But what would that have said to my mother, to my siblings? To those poor kids who didn't have a father anymore."

"But *you* didn't have a father anymore."

"At least I remembered him. My father was a good man, a hard worker. But it was that hard work that put him into an early grave. Massive heart attack probably brought on by stress. Thankfully, it was fast. If there's any phobia I have now, it's that I'm going to keel over without notice. I go to a doctor regularly; I don't smoke or drink, some of the byproducts of my upbringing. And no, I don't regret it. I see myself in you, Greco. Stoic, hardworking, but stubborn when it comes to asking for help. There always comes a time—I don't care how strong you are, how smart you are, or how well you think you have things put together—there's always a time to ask for help. Humility has a way of biting us in the ass. I think you know that by now, don't you, son?"

"Yes, Coach. I do. My butt feels like it's had a huge bite taken out of it."

Coach Grant chuckled. "Yeah. Losing by four touchdowns will do that to a man. But you see that team right there?" He pointed to a fading picture in the corner. "That team didn't win a game all season, but the last game we played was against the top team in the nation, and by then we were battered and bruised. It would've been easy for those kids to give up. I expected it. But there was one kid on the team, right there. You can see him in the second row." I wasn't sure, but I thought that a tear came to Coach's eye. "Pete Metcalf. Lanky wide receiver from California. He didn't have a lot of talent, but he sure worked hard. Somehow, some way, he rallied that team, and I'll be damned, when it came down to the wire, we beat that team, and you would've thought we had won the national championship. Those men had forged a bond that no one could ever break." His seriousness went to sadness. "I lost some of those boys to Vietnam. Pete Metcalf was the first. I was there when they gave the Silver Star to his parents. He saved his entire platoon, and all I could think about during his funeral was that last game, when the rest of his brothers rose to the occasion. I wondered what it was during that season that had sparked greatness in Pete Metcalf and how that spark had turned into a flame. That flame went with him to Vietnam and burned so bright that it saved thirty-nine men but had taken Pete with it. Because here's another thing, Greco. In life, sometimes shit happens. That I know you know. It wasn't fair your father died. It wasn't fair that he left his responsibility to take care of his family to you. But you can't change that now. And you can't do it alone, son."

"I understand, Coach."

"Do you, Greco? Because I want you to understand. I can say these words, and you can nod your head, but if you don't truly grasp the concept of reaching out your hand and asking for aid, I can't teach it to you. You must want it so damn bad that you do it for yourself. Now, is there anything else that you want to tell me? Anything I can help you with?"

I wanted to tell him everything. I wanted to tell him about Dad and everything he'd left to me, all the responsibilities, all the debts and deals, about Uncle Freddy and my mom, and about how Tommy was right now sleeping in my room, and that he'd been beaten up by somebody that we owed, but I didn't.

Instead, I said, "Thank you, Coach. If there's anything I think I should bring to your attention, I will."

I tried to ignore the look of disappointment on Coach Grant's face, but I wasn't ready. Not yet. My world had yet to become my nightmare.

Chapter 30

When I got back to the room, Tommy had turned my half into a pigsty. I was too tired to say anything. I handed him his breakfast and said, "Your bus leaves at five o'clock tonight."

I'd somehow scrounged up enough money for a bus ticket. Tommy barely acknowledged me, and Leroy caught my attention and pointed outside. He wanted to talk. I figured he'd probably tell me something like *Hey, your brother just can't just show up out of the blue. This is my room, too, you know.*

He closed the door and looked down the hallway. We were alone.

"Look, I'm really sorry about my brother."

He shook his head. "I don't care. He can stay as long as he needs to," Leroy said. That surprised me. It shouldn't have. Like I've said, Leroy was a good friend.

"What happened to his face?"

I wanted to tell him the truth. I really did, but this was part of my life where lies came easy because it covered up the painful open wounds.

"He got in a scrap with some boys back home." I think I did a pretty good job convincing him, because he didn't press.

"Are you sure he should go home?" Leroy asked.

"Yeah, I think that mess is over with. You know how it is when you're kids; you fight it out, and then you get over it."

Leroy nodded. "And how are you doing?" he asked. "You look tired."

"I'm okay," I lied.

"What about your girlfriend?"

"I'm not so sure she's my girlfriend."

Leroy's eyes went wide. "What did you do to screw it up?"

"Nothing, honest. I think she had her fill of me, is all."

"Are you crazy?" Leroy said.

"Hey, keep it down, okay?"

"I will not keep it down, Greco. There's something special about her, and you know it. When I saw you with her, something changed. There was a peace about you. Now, you know I'm not one to pry into someone's business, but with you . . ." He poked me in the chest. "I think you need somebody prying into your business."

"Hey, back off, okay?"

"No, I will not back off." He poked me in the chest again.

"What's your problem, man?"

"My problem is the fact that you're keeping secrets from me. I thought we were supposed to be friends."

"We are friends."

"Then why the secrets?"

"It's not that simple, okay?"

He crossed his arms and just stared at me. "You know, my mom says secrets lead you to an early grave."

"Yeah, well, I never heard that before," I said.

"Now you have."

"Listen, I've got it handled, okay—"

"Just leave you alone," he finished for me.

"That's not what I meant . . ." But he'd already turned and gone back into the room. "Leroy, hey . . ." He didn't listen. When I went back into the room, he had his headphones on and didn't look up, but Tommy did. He'd made a mess on my bed and asked, "Hey, you got any more food?"

◆ ◆ ◆

"Listen, stay out of trouble. Don't say anything that you're not supposed to. You got that?" We were at the bus station, and they'd called for all passengers.

"Yeah, I got it," Tommy said. Maybe if my words didn't sink in, then the split lip and bruised face would.

"Listen, we're in this together. I love you. You know that, right?" I asked.

"Hey, cut it out." He slapped my hand away. "I'm fine, all right?"

"Tommy . . ." He waved me away and got on the bus. I saw him take a seat halfway back. He looked once out the window and then slouched into his seat. There were only so many battles I could win. As I stood there watching the bus pull away, I hoped he would figure it out. But he was a knuckleheaded teenager who thought he knew the answers, that the world had done him wrong, so he was going to say and do everything back.

I had so much work to do that it made me want to bash my head against a wall, but I didn't go straight home. I knew where I had to go.

◆ ◆ ◆

Sheila's father answered the front door.

"Mr. Sinclair, I didn't realize . . ."

"Greco. Hi." He glanced back and then refocused on me. "Look, it's not exactly a good time."

"Is everything okay?" I asked quickly.

"Sure. Everything's fine. It's just that Sheila—"

"You can let him in, Dad."

"Honey . . ."

The sound of Sheila's voice cracked straight through my heart.

Mr. Sinclair said quietly so only I could hear, "Don't stay long, okay? She's feeling better, but she needs to rest."

Feeling better. Better from what? He led me into the house, up the stairs, and into the living room. Sheila was sitting next to her mother on the couch, wrapped in a blanket, and though she still looked beautiful, she looked exhausted.

"Hi," I said lamely.

"Hi," she answered, covering herself up as if embarrassed by the way she looked.

"Why don't we leave these two alone?" Claudia said, getting up from the couch. When she walked by me, she put a hand on my arm. "It's good to see you again, Greco."

"You, too, ma'am."

Sheila's parents disappeared, and there I stood in the middle of the living room, staring at a beautiful girl, not knowing what to say.

"How have you been?" Sheila asked.

"Okay," I said, with a shrug of shoulders.

"I heard about the game. I'm sorry."

"It's just one game," I said. "How about you? Are you doing okay?"

She ran a hand through her hair like the motion might get her a better answer than the one she'd prepared.

"Sure. I'm doing okay. Do you want to have a drink or something?"

"I'm fine, thanks. I wanted to come by and see you."

"I'm glad you did," she said. "I'm sorry I never called you back. I've been a little under the weather."

"Is it okay? I mean, are you feeling better?"

"I am, thanks," she said. She patted the couch next to her, and that's when I noticed the things on the table: the large empty bowl, the crumpled tissues, the orange bottle of pills.

She hugged me when I sat down, and I realized how fragile she felt, but she still smelled so good.

"I missed you," she said.

"I missed you too."

We stayed like that for I don't know how long. I could have remained in her embrace forever. Maybe she would fix every problem in my life, like all the crap about my dad and my family, if she just held me.

At some point, she released her grasp and looked up. There was something in her eyes that I couldn't decipher, and then the preamble began. I could hear my heart crack when she said, "Greco, there's something I need to tell you."

Chapter 31

"I couldn't call you because I was in Switzerland."

"Switzerland?" I asked.

Sheila nodded. "There's a doctor in Zurich. He's the best in the world. He's been—"

"Wait, a doctor? You are sick."

Sheila looked away, but I put my hand on the side of her face and turned her back.

"Please tell me," I said.

"I'm sorry I got you into this," Sheila said. She was crying now. "But that night when we first met, I saw you, and I can't explain it. I wanted you. I wanted to be with you. You looked so innocent and full of, I don't know, life, I guess. But at the same time, you looked scared, and I wanted to hold you. It's stupid, I know. I should have just gotten a beer and walked away."

"I'm glad you didn't," I said.

"Greco, you don't mean that."

"Of course I do." I held both of her hands now. "Listen, whatever it is, I'm not going anywhere, okay?"

"Greco, you're a freshman. You've wonderful years ahead of you. And I . . ."

"What?" I asked. "What is it?"

She explained that it was an aggressive type of cancer. Something in her blood. This would sap away her strength and leave her as helpless as a newborn.

"I feel fine most of the time," Sheila said. "But then, I have these fits. That's what Mom calls them. Dad's worried. That's why they're here. Oh, Greco, I shouldn't have pulled you into this. I wouldn't be mad if you left right now, I promise. Go live your life without me. I'll be fine. I've got my parents."

This was one of those pivotal moments in my life where it would've been easy to take the low road. Funny thing was I didn't have to try. My answer was easy.

"I'm glad you talked to me that night. You intimidated the hell out of me. You were gorgeous. You are gorgeous."

She blushed and nestled her face on my chest. "Oh, Greco. How are we going to make this work?"

"I don't know, but we'll figure it out. I promise."

I never should have made that promise, but again, it's something that you say and need desperately to believe for the people you love. And yeah, I knew I loved her, impossible as it sounds. What had it been, a few weeks? This woman had gotten me hook, line, and sinker.

"Can I get *you* something to drink?" I asked.

She looked up at me, that beautiful smile finally playing on her lips. "Do you remember where the wine cellar is?"

I nodded.

"Bring the dustiest bottle. I think I can afford a little splurge, don't you?"

Chapter 32

Sheila got through half her glass of wine and fell asleep on me. I sat there for a time. At some point, her mother appeared.

"I should get her to bed," she said. She rubbed her daughter's back, and Sheila woke.

"Did I fall asleep?" she asked.

"It's okay," I said. "I need to get back. Lots of fun freshman homework."

Sheila nodded and kissed me on the cheek, then left with her mother wordlessly.

"Can I give you a ride back to the dorms?" Mr. Sinclair asked.

"If it wouldn't be an imposition," I said.

"Not at all. I was going to pick up some things at the grocery store. You're on my way."

I wished the convertible's top was down as we drove. I needed the fresh air to clear my brain. I closed my eyes and imagined a world where everything was perfect, a world where Sheila was healthy, where my arm threw exactly the way it was supposed to. A world where my brain picked up on what lessons I was supposed to learn and my heart opened up to my friends.

"Greco, I want to thank you for being so kind to my daughter," Mr. Sinclair said. I opened my eyes and saw that he was gripping the wheel hard, at exactly ten and two.

"Yes, sir," I said.

He turned and looked at me.

"We've done the best we can, and I wouldn't say this around my wife, and I don't mean to scare you. I'm scared. She's my daughter, my only child. You'll understand one day, Greco, when you have kids of your own."

"Yes, sir," I said.

"I hope you don't mind, but we overheard what she told you. She gave you an out, and you decided to stay. I don't think that after you've had a night to sleep on it that she would hold it against you if you did indeed change your mind."

"Sir, I'm not going to change my mind."

"I thought so," he said, his voice catching. "I don't know what we're going to do. It's getting worse." He wiped a hand across his eyes. "Look at me. You barely know me, and I'm crying."

"It's okay," I said. I didn't feel comfortable putting a hand on his shoulder or anything like that, so I tried to listen. "Do you think this doctor in Switzerland will figure it out?" I asked.

Mr. Sinclair shrugged.

"I don't know. He is the best, and if it weren't for him, she wouldn't be at school right now."

"Why don't you take her home to New York?"

Mr. Sinclair laughed. "You don't think we've tried? I'd love nothing more, but Sheila is her own woman, and I have to respect this is where she wants to be. She wants to finish her master's degree. She wants to live life. I can't take that from her, Greco."

"Yes, sir. I think I understand."

"I believe you do, son." He pulled up to the dorm and reached into his pocket, pulled out his wallet, opened it, and handed me a business card. "This is my number. If Sheila ever needs anything, call me, please."

I took the card, hoping that I would never have to use it, but he grabbed my arm so forcefully that I had to look straight into his eyes. "Greco, you think about what she said. This isn't a burden I would give any man. Do you understand that?"

"Yes, sir. I understand."

But I didn't understand, not truly. I got out of the car and walked slowly up to my dorm. I looked at the business card. It said "David Sinclair, The Sinclair Foundation." On the other side was his number. I thought about going for a walk to clear my head, but there was too much to do. Something about Sheila's revelation had spurred me to action. I promised myself that I would get all my work done. I would be the best student, the best quarterback, the best boyfriend I could be. Somehow, I'd figure it all out. I was almost nineteen, but I'd been a man for a long time.

I looked up at the sky, and for the first time in a long time, I said a prayer, hoping to have a man-to-man talk with God. But as I stood there staring up at the sky, no answers came, no solutions, no epiphanies. And when I looked down, I realized that I was alone, that I would have to do this myself. At least that's what I thought, because I still didn't know any better.

Chapter 33

As strange as it sounds, Sheila's sickness made everything work. I got into a routine. Where before, it felt like my days owned me, now I owned them. I had a purpose.

I was quick and snappy at practice, and even the big offensive lineman, Wilbur Downs, nodded at me a couple of times—the ultimate sign of respect. But that still didn't keep him from growling when I screwed up, which happened more than he liked.

Every day after practice, Coach and I had a private meeting. He wanted to make sure my head was on straight and I hadn't taken any unnecessary hits. I didn't blame him. We were still looking for backup quarterbacks. Pip had a decent arm, but he didn't have the size. Besides, he was quickly overtaking the starting kicker and becoming known as *the* man despite his country-club looks. Pip could stare down the jaws of a convergent defense and never flinch as he kicked the ball.

I got ahead on schoolwork. I started planning my classes for the next semester. This time I would be smarter. I went to my adviser, and she showed me exactly which classes I could take if I wanted to fit them in with spring practice and my new major, which I thought would be business administration. I thought about doing psychology like Sheila. But when I perused the course offerings for a track in psychology, I only saw one class that really piqued my interest.

We started winning games again by large margins. We were touted nationally as the resurgent Jefferson State team. There were talks of going to a bowl game, and you have to remember, back then there weren't 101 bowl games like there are today. It was a right you earned.

Rolling into November, I had a steady girlfriend. I had a 3.4 GPA. I was close to taking the title of most accurate quarterback in the league. I was becoming known for my fifty-yard stingers. Yeah, you could say things were going well. I'd invited my mom and Tommy to the game before Thanksgiving. Then I'd meet them at home, and I'd spend most of my week there. I was trying to figure out how to sneak away and spend some time with Sheila. She was going to New York, and I figured I could surprise her. I'd call her dad, and we'd work out the reveal together. I'd seen them often and enjoyed spending time with the Sinclair family. There was a steadiness in them that I'd never experienced in my own life.

Things were peachy keen as I walked to class on Friday, the day before our biggest game of the season, the one that might put us into the conference championship. The student body knew me by now, and as I walked to class with Leroy, people would call out, "Hey, there's Greco!"

"Good luck, Greco!"

"Lee Roy Jack-Son!" some of them would chant, and Leroy would dance around in a circle, arms in the air like Rocky.

"This is me," Leroy said, giving me a high five and peeling off to the right. Our friendship was stronger than ever.

I went left and was making my way to the building where I had my next class when a car horn honked. I turned my head.

"You've got to be kidding me," I said under my breath.

Uncle Freddy waved from the car. I thought about waving back and then running. But what the hell would that get me? Jerk was probably wondering why I hadn't invited him to the game. Reluctantly, I walked over to the car.

"There he is," Uncle Freddy said. "The big bad quarterback who's taking over the league. How you doing, nephew?"

"Fine," I said. "But I've got to get to class."

"Class, aye? You doing well in school?"

"I am," I said.

"Good. That's good. I wouldn't want you to lose your place as starting quarterback."

"I've got to get to class, Uncle Freddy."

"Sure, sure."

What the hell was he beating around the bush for? Usually, he was Mr. Straight to the Point.

"Listen, I've been taking care of your mother, but she's got expensive tastes. Always wants to go out for a steak, have a couple of drinks. Hell, you know the last time we went out cost me fifty bucks. Fifty bucks, Greco! You think I can just throw fifty bucks around?"

I knew very well that it was easy for Uncle Freddy to throw way more than fifty bucks if he was in a poker game.

"That's not my problem, Uncle Freddy."

"That's where you're wrong, nephew. It *is* your problem. You see, my cash reserves are dwindling, as they say in the banking industry."

Uncle Freddy didn't know a damn thing about banks other than the fact that they were places that held money, much like the nook under his mattress.

"Here's what you're going to do, nephew. You've got a big game tomorrow, right?"

I nodded.

"I'm going to put some money on the game, a good chunk of money, but your team is favored to win by a touchdown. My bookie is trying to put the screws to me. You understand?"

I understood that he probably owed this bookie thousands of dollars and that he was trying to play the angle, and I knew exactly where this was going.

"Here's what I need you to do, nephew. I need you to keep it close, like real close. And when everybody thinks it's over, and I hate to say this because I really have enjoyed all the articles in the newspaper, but Jefferson State University will lose that game."

"I can't do that," I said, my tone firm and uncompromising.

Uncle Freddy nodded like he wasn't upset in the least.

"I understand. I understand. A boy's got to do what a boy's got to do. Am I right?"

I didn't answer.

"But here's the thing, Greco, I know people. You hear? Those people that send you those faxes? I know all about them. You're coming up on the end, aren't you? Here's the deal, the right whispers in the right ears, I can make that go on forever. It'll make a lost game seem like a bee sting. When in fact, you better be ready to be fucked by a rhino."

"Did you come up with that one on your own, or did you read it in the cartoons?" I asked.

"Take your pick." He was grinning, rubbing his knuckles like he was warming up for a fight.

"Do you understand, nephew?"

"Yes, I understand."

"Good. Now get to class. I wouldn't want you to get behind."

He put the car in drive, stuck his hand out the window, and waved to me as he drove off. What I wouldn't have given for a rocket launcher or a bit of napalm in that very moment.

Chapter 34

Mom phoned and told me that they would get there early, that she'd like to see me before the game, to give me a hug for good luck. I told her that there was no way, that Coach was making us get to the field early to start warm-ups. That was a lie, but I didn't want to take the chance that she would be with Uncle Freddy. I'd only given Mom two tickets—one for her and one for Tommy—and they were waiting at the stadium.

The night before, I'd studied tape with the rest of the team. It was going to be a hard fight. Uncle Freddy's threat swished and squirmed in my mind as I analyzed the angles I might take to cobble together another win for our team. The funny thing was I wasn't scared. I analyzed each and every angle the way I analyzed the football field. I thought about contingencies. I thought about getting hurt. I thought about winning the game by six touchdowns. I thought about losing the game by three. I thought about telling my team. I thought about telling Coach. I thought about telling Mom.

I did none of those things. I kept it all inside.

The stadium was buzzing when our team ran out onto the field. I could feel the electricity in the air. The marching band boomed, and students cheered. The cheerleaders did flips and twirls and led the crowd in chants. I don't know what it was about the way I carried myself that night, but everybody gave me space. They all probably figured that I was stone-cold focused, and I was. And I'm going to tell you something here. I don't brag—it's not worth my time—but that first quarter, we took the field and smashed our opponent right in the face. I threw for one touchdown and ran in for two more. We were up 21–0 going into the second quarter.

By then, our opponent had regained some of its footing. Leroy was called in. And on his first play, he intercepted the ball and ran it back for a touchdown, his first of the year.

I let the rest of the team congratulate him. I was too focused on my next set of plays. I hadn't even looked into the crowd, though I could imagine Mom and Tommy standing, cheering for me. It was 28–0.

On their next possession, the other team scored. Now it was 28–7. Our offense took the field, and I was on a roll again, right down the field, but one of my wide receivers bobbled the ball, and before it hit the ground, the other team scooped it up and ran it back to midfield, then in a succession of plays ran it into the end zone.

The score was now 28–14.

I don't know if you've ever been on a field or a court. When the tide starts to turn, you can feel it, like the current shifting underneath you in the ocean. It doesn't so much feel like a riptide but a slow pulling in the opposite direction. I felt it then. In fact, I could feel everything. I glanced at the crowd and saw Mom and Tommy. They waved to me, but I didn't wave back, because right behind Mom was Uncle Freddy. He wasn't smiling; he was glaring, and I knew what that meant.

More bad luck on our next possession. This time we did get in the end zone, but as our running back dove across the line, he was smashed in the side, jostling the ball. When it came down and the pile was uncovered, the ball was in the other team's possession. A turnover that led to yet another opponent touchdown.

We went to the locker room at halftime up 28–21. I did not look up into the stands when we left the field. At the half, Coach talked about keeping control of the ball. He talked about the things we were doing right and told us to do more of them. There was never any of that rah-rah nonsense from Coach Grant. He looked each and every one of us in the eye like a man, and we felt a deep responsibility to never let him down.

What happened in the third quarter was a battle of the offenses. I was a madman, steel focused and tough to take down. I kicked and clawed my way for more yardage. I threw passes that seemed impossible but were caught in soft hands.

Each team put another twenty-one points on the board. By the fourth quarter, you could tell that each side was going to leave everything out on that field. It was the last quarter; our defenses took over. Back and forth we battled, neither team able to pick up a first down. Punts became puny returns. Passes flew incomplete. Runs became losses. Tackles became brawls.

We were still up by one touchdown, and I almost laughed when I looked at the scoreboard. Four minutes left, and our opponent had the ball.

Their running game was stronger than ours, but I could pick them apart in the air. And just like that, I felt a snap of tension release. I knew in that moment that I could do anything. These days we call it finding the flow, or getting in the zone.

As I watched tight lipped, we gave up another touchdown, and when I looked up to the stands, I saw Uncle Freddy cheering.

Okay, let's go, I thought.

The kickoff resulted in our returner taking a knee. We were on our own twenty yard line with less than three minutes to go. It looked to everyone else like a long way to go, but to me, the field felt wide open. And sure enough, when the center put the ball into my hands and I dropped back to pass, everyone else looked slow and sluggish. But not me. I saw every hole, every opening. Knuckles wrapped in bloody tape. Eyes wide in bloodshot concentration. Spittle flying from open-mouthed helmets.

My first pass was a first down fifteen-yard completion. The next play Coach called was a pass. Instead of passing it, I took it around the left side, picking up eleven yards and another first down. We were almost in midfield when the whistles blew, signaling that we had two minutes left.

I jogged to the sideline and faced Coach Grant.

He looked at me and said, "Do you know what to do, Greco?"

I said, "Yes, Coach, I do."

I didn't need water; I didn't need a towel. I did not need to look up into the stands. I needed the football.

We were tied, and with a tie, Uncle Freddy would probably win some money, but what he wanted was for us to lose. When I got to the line, I did glance up into the stands, and when I caught Uncle Freddy's eye, I gave him a little salute. He frowned. I dropped back. My center spun the ball into my hands. The pocket was strong, led by Wilbur Downs. My offensive linemen were doing their job and doing it to perfection. I probably could have stood there for a good thirty seconds, but I didn't need that long. I saw what I needed, and he was crossing the thirty, the twenty-five, the twenty . . .

I let the ball fly, knowing it would go exactly where I wanted. The ball dropped down a yard into the end zone, exactly where I'd calculated, exactly where my wide receiver was running, exactly where he'd be wide open because he'd outrun his defender.

There was only one problem. As my receiver took the first step into the end zone, a defender came out of nowhere. And as the ball hit one hand of the receiver, the collision of the two men sounded like a car crash and elicited an "Ooooooh" from the crowd.

The ball flipped up into the air, and all I could do was watch. Our wide receiver fell to the ground, cradling an injured arm. When the ball came down, it was in the other team's hands. To the ten he ran, then the fifteen, and the twenty.

The chase was on, and I was part of it. The interceptor slipped through one, two, three of our men. I was the one who finally took him out at the fifty, and when he got up, he flicked the ball in my face and said, "Clean that off for me, will you, boy?"

I ran back to the sideline. I knew what I had to do. Coach was talking to the defense, really firing them up. I grabbed his arm and turned him toward me. "Coach, I need to go in."

"Greco, it's the defense's turn."

"Coach, you don't understand. I need to go in."

He turned and faced me. I don't know what he saw, maybe he saw desperation. Maybe he saw determination. Maybe he saw a kid who was desperate to make up for his last act.

He spoke to the team. "Greco's in. Peterson, you're out."

There seemed to be some confusion among the defense, but nobody questioned Coach. We went back out on the field, and for the first two plays, it felt strange to be back on defense. It took me a minute to get my bearings, though I could still see everything happening on the field. The other team got a first down. With less than a minute to go, they needed either a touchdown or a field goal. I figured either one would put Uncle Freddy in the black, but I wasn't going to let that happen. I couldn't let that happen.

On the next play, one of their linemen on their strong side lost his footing, and I pushed him the rest of the way to the ground, then swam my way past the next blocker, earning a wide hole toward the quarterback.

His eyes met mine. I saw his eyes flicker right, and I knew what was coming. I timed it perfectly. He let the ball launch, and I was already in the air. The ball hit my hands, and I sure as hell wasn't going to let it go. I came down with it, legs already moving.

Their quarterback tried to take me down, but I bulled through him and ran for everything I had. I'm not sure why this next thing hit me in that moment, but what I felt like I was running for most was my dad. He was imperfect. He was probably a criminal. He was many things, but he was still my dad.

As I chugged down the field, I heard him next to me, "Run, son, run."

And I ran.

And when I stepped foot into the end zone, I went down to my knees, cradling that ball in my hands as time ran out, and my team swarmed me, followed by the rest of the student body.

When I was hoisted into the air and my eyes scanned the crowd, I found him, Uncle Freddy, standing all alone in his seat, glaring at me, promising that my good deed would not go unpunished.

Chapter 35

The celebration went on long into the night. Everyone wanted to shake my hand or give me a pat on the back. When we walked by the bars, the bouncers offered me free drinks, but I laughed and said we were going to another party.

We made the rounds, me, Pip, and Leroy. They basically had to act as my bodyguards, keeping people at arm's length, making sure we didn't stay in any place too long. It was Leroy's plan, like we were running for office and hitting the home of each and every constituent.

I wished on a few occasions that Sheila were there, but she was already in New York with her parents.

I received two surprises that night. When we stopped at Wilbur Downs's fraternity house, of all the places, he offered me a beer as soon as I walked in the door. I took it, and he offered his hand. "That was a ballsy move, Greco. Real ballsy."

"Thanks," I said, not trusting the way he was looking at me with so much heart-warming intensity.

"Come on. I want to introduce you to everyone."

Leroy and Pip both gave me a look like *Holy shit, is this really happening?*

Downs treated us like honored guests. Not only me, who he introduced as "his quarterback," but Leroy, who he introduced as his "little brother." He said that next season Leroy was going to give the running backs a run for their money and Pip, though he looked like a preppy tennis star, was going to one day go to the NFL with his super leg.

The next surprise was when Coach Grant showed up, and no, he did not share a beer with his football players. He did not give us a look like *Hey, you're only eighteen. What are you drinking beer for?* He came to congratulate us and to tell us to enjoy the night, that we deserved it. But he did pull me aside and say, "Greco, what happened tonight won't happen again. Understand?"

"Yes, Coach, I understand, and I'm sorry."

"No need to apologize, son, you did what you thought was right. You were a leader out there today. Now, go enjoy yourself."

He left quietly, and another round of revelers showed up. Downs had to tell them one more time how his crazy quarterback had decided to play on defense and save the day. Not that those students hadn't been there, but it turned out that Downs, when he'd had a few beers, was quite the storyteller. He punctuated the retelling with a booming laugh.

The night was through. We were walking back to the dorms, and I had almost forgotten about Uncle Freddy. Almost. I expected to see him at any turn, but bolstered by alcohol and surrounded by friends, I figured it was a small chance. He never made an appearance.

I went to bed still in my clothes, definitely not something that I usually did or have done since. I was refreshingly exhausted and more than a little drunk. I thought about calling Sheila before going to sleep, but I didn't want to wake her. I would call her the next morning.

I woke up with a margin of the excitement from the night before, but my head was pounding, and my stomach was turning twists.

I had to call Sheila. Before I reached for the phone, my eyes went to the fax. A short fax had come in. I leaned over, groaning as my body grumbled. The fax was not encoded. It said simply "We need to talk." There was no signature, no phone number, no anything. And when I looked in the mirror, I knew that my suddenly pale face had nothing to do with the alcohol the night before. It had everything to do with the fact that the man or men behind the scenes were displeased with my actions. And now, days before Thanksgiving, it would be time for me to pay the piper.

Chapter 36

I hitched a ride home with a girl who lived in the next dorm over. I think she liked Leroy and didn't mind going a little bit out of her way to take me with her. I had her drop me in the middle of the town, and I thought about walking the opposite way. Instead, I reluctantly went home.

Mom was there to greet me, and lo and behold, she was stone-cold sober. She was dressed up like it was Easter. She'd put makeup on. She looked like a normal mom.

"Where's Tommy?" I asked once she finished fawning over me.

"He's out with some friends. You know Tommy."

I did know Tommy, and I was worried that he was out getting in trouble. I asked my mom about Tommy's grades and how he was doing with his teachers.

She pooh-poohed it all and said, "You know him. He's not as much for grades as you were, but he's enjoying football."

She told me how they'd won a few games, but I could tell by the way she was talking she really had no clue. Maybe Tommy had mentioned it to her in passing. At least she was done up nice and the house was picked up. I was about to ask about my uncle Freddy and how much time he'd been spending at the house when there was a knock at the door.

"Why don't you get that, honey?" Mom said. "I'll make you some lunch."

That was a change. I tossed my duffel onto the couch and went to the front door.

There was another knock, and I called out, "I'm coming."

I opened the front door to find a squat man with beady eyes. He wore a suit, a collared shirt underneath—not a button-down—and no tie.

"Michael Greco?" he asked.

I half expected him, in his gravelly voice, to pull a gun from his waistband and stick it in my stomach.

"I'm Greco," I said.

I flinched when he actually reached into his pocket, but he pulled out a small envelope and handed it to me. Without another word, he walked back to the street, got into the black Lincoln that was idling, and chugged off.

I looked down at the envelope. I knew exactly what this was. I'd been told to come home. Ordered to come home. So this was likely my next set of instructions.

I opened the envelope and pulled out the small card. It said simply "Be available." I tore up the card, went back inside, flushed the remnants of the card and the envelope down the toilet, and went to my room.

I don't know what I expected. An immediate summoning? An executioner at my door?

The week dragged on, and I relived all the joys of being home— Mom drinking too much, slurring, barely being able to keep the stove from setting the house on fire. I took over all household duties: cooking, cleaning, laundry. I didn't leave. I didn't go to the high school. I didn't go to the bank. I didn't see any of my friends. When I wasn't playing houseman, I pulled out my books and did my best to prepare for my upcoming finals.

Here's the thing. When doom's looming over you, it's hard to study. You know what I mean? I'm not sure if any book knowledge sank into my bothered brain.

For Thanksgiving, I told Mom we were reviving an old tradition. Like on television, I would get Chinese food, and we'd have a feast. She complained and said she wanted turkey. Good thought . . . but she wasn't going to cook a turkey, and I sure as hell didn't know how to cook one.

It was noon on Thanksgiving Day. I was writing down exactly what I was going to order from the Chinese restaurant. It was a short walk from the house, and I figured I could get there and back in ten, fifteen minutes, tops. I didn't get the chance.

The phone rang, and I answered it, "Greco residence."

"There's a car outside. Get in it."

The call ended, and it felt like someone poured ice water in my veins.

"Honey, was that the Chinese place?" Mom called out from the living room where she was downing Carlo Rossi by the pint.

I bit back my nerves, walked into the living room, and said, "I'm going to run out to the store."

"The car keys are on the counter."

"That's okay, Mom. I'll walk."

Tommy was in his room, where he had been since I had gotten home. He pretty much avoided me, and that was fine. I went outside and saw the car that was waiting for me, a throwback Cadillac, black, with tinted windows. I walked to the car and had visions of tommy gun–wielding muscle popping out of the doors and spraying me with bullets. In my mind they'd leave my body lifeless on the front stoop. Good news: no machine guns emerged. I knocked on the window. It rolled down. It was the same squat guy from earlier in the week.

"Get in the back," he said.

I got in the back seat, closed the door, and asked, "Where are we going?"

"On the seat next to you. There's a hood. Put it on."

I grabbed the black hood and hesitated. He was looking at me in the rearview mirror.

"Put it on," he said.

He sounded bored, like he did this twenty times a day. I put the hood over my head, glad to find that it smelled not like the nervous sweat of nineteen predecessors but like clean laundry. I felt the car pull away from the curb, and I wondered if this was the last time I would see home.

Chapter 37

I want you to play a little game. Imagine you're in the back of a car that belongs to someone you don't know. You've got a hood over your head. You can't see anything. Now imagine how you'd feel.

Here's the deal. You can't unless you've been there.

I tried to stay calm. But terror makes the body do all sorts of involuntary things, like shudder, shake, and twitch. I went through four versions of escape in my head: busting out the door, busting out the window, jumping over the seat, and trying to strangle the squat guy, although his neck was so thick, I didn't think I could get my hands around it. Then I reminded myself that it was no use, that I should sit there and wait.

I clasped my hands in my lap, grabbed my thighs, then squeezed them. I tapped on my knees as we took turn after turn, the driver saying nothing.

We finally, mercifully, came to a stop, and the driver said, "Don't move."

Here it comes, I thought.

Would I feel the cold muzzle pressed to my temple, or would it be like in *The Godfather*, where somebody'd wrap a garrote around my neck and squeeze until I was dead, Luca Brasi–style?

There was no gun, and there was no garrote.

Someone opened the door and pulled me out with strong hands. They were gentle but forceful.

"Watch your step," a new voice said.

I was slowly guided up a set of stairs.

I heard a door opening, and then the smell of cigarette smoke and home cooking filled my senses.

I thought I heard murmuring but couldn't tell.

There was music playing. I recognized '50s or '60s throwbacks.

I'm pretty sure I heard a set of sliding doors open. I was marched in, and the sliding doors closed behind me. I was pushed down into a chair, again gently, and the voice that had taken me out of the car said, "Stay here."

Again, the sound of sliding doors and then stomping away. I could make out the faint music behind me. I smelled cigarette smoke, or maybe the remnants.

I'm not sure how long I waited there. It could have been five minutes. It could have been fifty. All the while, my heart hammered in my chest.

Then came the sound of sliding doors again, and footsteps. I heard the flick of a lighter and the telltale crackle of a cigarette being sucked.

"You can take your hood off," the voice said.

It was all I could do not to rip it off my head. I took it off slowly and squinted at the light, though it was dim in the room. It was like a sitting room. There were bookcases along the far wall, with windows on either side. The curtains were closed, keeping it dark and cave-like.

A man sat across from me on the other side of a coffee table. His skin was stretched across his skull, more macabre Halloween costume than actual man, I thought. I knew exactly who this man was: Giancarlo Romano, but everyone knew him as Johnny Cheese. You figure that one out. But nobody called him that to his face, at least not anymore. Maybe in the old days. I'd only met Mr. Romano once, and, of course, I'd been with my dad. It was at a ball game. I'd never seen Dad be so respectful. I swear he would've bowed and kissed the man's feet if he had been allowed.

"You know who I am," Mr. Romano said. His accent was barely noticeable.

He was wearing a tailored suit that looked like it was two sizes too big. I could see that the cut was good, but for some reason it didn't fit him well. And that's when I realized he was either sick or had recently been through an illness. I don't know why that seemed important at the time. Maybe it was my mind gathering clues.

"Yes, Mr. Romano, I know who you are."

"Good. Tell me, how is school?"

This guy was asking me about school. Then what? A bullet to the head?

"School is good. I think I figured out the class part."

"Football?"

I shrugged. He set the cigarette down on the ashtray on the coffee table.

"You'll have to excuse me. I don't follow football. I've always been a baseball fan. Much like your father, no?"

"Yes, sir."

"Your father was a good man, or at least he tried to be, but he was useful for a time."

He let that comment sit, and he stared at me, and I did my best to match his gaze. I don't know how I did it.

"I apologize for my appearance," he said finally. "I have not been well, but the doctors and their needles seem to have fixed me. My sister has promised a large feast for Thanksgiving to fatten me up again."

When he smiled, he looked like a leering skeleton, and I did my best not to wince and crawl inside myself.

"I'm glad you're feeling better, sir," I said.

At first, he didn't reply, and then he tapped the side of his nose. "Why do I think that you actually mean that?"

I figured it was a rhetorical question, and I didn't answer.

"I have guests coming. I won't keep you. Let's get to the point of your visit." He sucked long and deep on the cigarette, as if he hadn't had one in ten years. "Certain allegations have been made. Up until this point, you've done well settling your father's debts. My friends tell me that you've acted honorably, and for that, you have my congratulations. But what we cannot tolerate is deception. And it has been brought to my attention that the full breadth of your father's business affairs have not been well communicated. Is that the case?"

I shook my head vigorously. "No, Mr. Romano, I promise."

He nodded, as if taking that into consideration. "I don't mean to call you a liar," he said, "but these dealings must be cared for in a judicious manner. Do you understand?"

"Yes, sir," I said.

"Good. When do you leave for school?"

"Sunday, Mr. Romano."

"That is perfect. Let us say you come to the morning eight o'clock mass. We'll figure this out in sight of God and his witnesses."

"Yes, sir," I said.

He was rising, and I got up out of my chair too. He walked around the table and shook my hand. His hand was more claw than human flesh.

"And Michael, don't forget to bring your father's ledger. I'm sure with its help, we can get everything sorted out."

I stood frozen to the spot as the doors behind me slid open and someone put the hood back over my head. I was whisked away, this time with less gentleness, as if to say *We know how to be nice, but we also know how to make things happen.*

Chapter 38

I was waiting outside the bank before it opened. A surly security guard who looked like he'd had his good time on Thanksgiving unlocked the front door and told me to wait. It took him a good fifteen minutes to do whatever the hell he was doing inside. Finally, he unlocked the door again and waved me in.

I looked around for Mrs. Mockingham. When I didn't see her, I went to a guy in a brown suit sitting at the desk, clacking away on a typewriter. He didn't look up from his pecking. "May I help you?" he asked.

"Is Mrs. Mockingham in today?"

"No, sorry. She's on vacation."

"That's okay," I said, trying not to sound too desperate. "I need to get into my safe-deposit box."

"Why don't you have a seat over there, and I'll be right with you."

Right with you meant another thirty minutes of clacking away on the typewriter. Meanwhile, nobody else lifted a finger to help me. I didn't want to go over to any of the tellers and disrespect the man who said he was going to help. With a flourish that might've made the New York Symphony conductor proud, Brown Suit yanked the sheet of paper from the typewriter, looking very pleased with himself. He sat it on the desk, got up from his chair, and walked over to me.

"I'm sorry for the wait," he said pleasantly. "This way, please."

We went through the usual routine. He asked for my identification, verified it with the bank's records, and then took me to the back. I watched as he inserted the key and pulled the safe-deposit box out, and then he escorted me to the private room.

"Come out when you've finished," he said.

"Yes, sir. Thank you."

I sat down at the tiny desk and waited a few moments. I'd gone back and forth about whether I should give Mr. Romano the ledger. Dad had been explicit with his instructions. "Don't let anyone see it. Keep it safe."

What the hell was I supposed to do? The most powerful man in my orbit wanted it, and who was I to say no? Maybe if I gave it to him, everything would be done. He would confirm that I was doing exactly as I'd been instructed with all the faxes. There was nothing I was hiding. I just wanted to be done.

I pretty much knew that it was Uncle Freddy who'd pointed the finger at me. Well, I'd show him. If the ledger was my trump card, screw it. I didn't need it anymore. Let them deal with it. At least that's what I hoped.

When I handed the ledger to Romano or whoever he wanted me to give it to at the morning mass, that would be it. Then we'd shake hands, and I would be on my way back to school, maybe never to come back again, because Thanksgiving had been a real shit show.

Mom had gotten stumbling drunk, muttering about how little we respected her and that if she'd had the choice, she would've had a girl. She'd slapped Tommy, who'd cocked a fist, and I swear he would have punched her in the face if I hadn't jumped in the middle. Then he'd run away and hadn't come back. I stayed up until well past midnight. Mom was snoring on the couch. I was pacing the living room floor. I could have taken the family car, a beat-up old Chevy that looked like no model I had ever seen or heard of since. I figured Tommy would slink back at some point, but he never did. Where did he go?

I breathed in and then out and reached over and opened the box. Let's get this over with, I thought.

I opened the lid of the box and reached inside.

One huge freaking problem.

The safe-deposit box was empty.

Chapter 39

It took a good ten minutes to slap my nerves back into submission. And even then, when I went and talked to Brown Suit again, I'm pretty sure my hands were shaking in my pockets.

"When did you say Mrs. Mockingham would be back?" I asked.

"I didn't," he said. He was going to be a hard case.

"Is there any way you can check and see who was the last person to open that box?"

"What are you insinuating, son?" he asked.

"Nothing. It's just that . . ." I didn't want to tell him my business. He had no right to know. "Thank you," I said quickly and hurried from the bank. I had two days to figure out what to do.

Sunday morning at eight o'clock, I had to see Mr. Romano, like he said, before God and all his witnesses. I didn't exactly know what that meant. Did that mean that he was going to clear out the church, and I was going to walk in, and there would be a ceremony for me? No. That was my mind running away. Church was a safe place, a public place to meet and nothing more. I had to keep telling myself that.

"Think, Greco," I told myself.

I needed to find Mrs. Mockingham. Then she could tell me, or at least I hoped she would, who had gotten access to the safe-deposit box and taken Dad's ledger, my insurance. But where did she live? Was she really on vacation?

I ran to the drugstore, where I knew there was a phone booth and a phone book. Yes, kids. Back in 1989, there was a book where you could look up people's phone numbers and addresses. The one in this particular phone booth had been graffitied, but apparently, ripping out the pages was beyond the artist's expertise.

I went straight to *M*—Madison, Maleschwitz, Maynard, and there it was, Mockingham. Three listings. I called the first number, and there was no answer. Someone at the second number answered, but it was an older woman who said nobody from the bank lived there. With the third, I hit the jackpot. Mrs. Mockingham answered.

"Hello?" she said.

"Mrs. Mockingham, it's Michael Greco." I heard jostling on the other end.

"I'm sorry," she said. "I have to go."

"No, Mrs. Mockingham, wait."

"I have to go."

The call ended, and I stared down at the receiver. I ripped the page out of the phone book (sorry to anybody who was looking for *Mo* last names in 1989). I didn't recognize her address, so I had to go into the drugstore and ask if I could look at a map.

The bored cashier said, "Sure, go ahead." She was half-asleep, and I probably could have done it without asking, but manners are manners. I found the right street and calculated how long it would take to run there. No time like the present.

I arrived at the Mockingham residence covered in sweat, despite the fact that it was a cold morning. The Mockingham lawn was perfectly manicured and rimmed with frost. There was a wood-paneled station wagon in the driveway, and a sign on the front door said WELCOME.

I rang the doorbell. No one answered. I rang the doorbell again and thought I caught movement in the side window. I knocked on the door and said, "Please, Mrs. Mockingham, it's Michael Greco."

Still no answer.

I couldn't remember whether she was married, or whether her husband was still alive, or whether they might have guns in the house, but I was desperate. I went around to the side of the house, then to the back. Everyone had a back door with a metal screen door as the first line of defense. The screen door was unlocked, so I opened it and knocked on the back door.

"Mrs. Mockingham, please."

More movement from inside and then a muted thump sound.

I tried the door handle, but it was locked.

I knocked again.

"Please, Mrs. Mockingham, I need your help." No more movement. I tried looking through the window, but everything was dark, so I went to the side and did the same, cupping my hands like window binoculars.

Still nothing.

Back to the front yard, I tried the doorbell one last time, but there was no answer. But when I looked through the side window, I saw feet. I panicked. I did the only thing I knew to do. I put my shoulder into the door, and luckily it burst in. Of course, I was young and strong, but most likely the door gave because it was old and weak.

The first thing I noticed was a smell like burnt fish. My eyes went to the stove where a pan was overcooking in smoky bellows. Then in my peripheral vision, I noticed the feet. I walked a couple of steps down the hall and saw that the feet were attached to ankles and legs and the body of Mrs. Mockingham, lying on the ground, a bottle of pills in her hand, and more pills scattered on the floor. She was face down.

I rolled her over tentatively. She was unconscious.

I put my ear to her chest and felt that she was barely breathing. Stupid me. I didn't know what CPR was. I ran to the phone and dialed 911. I had to pull out the sheet of phone book paper to give them the address, though they could probably track it back then.

"Please hurry," I said. I thought about leaving. When I went into the living room, there was white foam coming out of Mrs. Mockingham's mouth.

"Somebody help, please," I called out. I sat her up and rested her against me, not wanting her to choke on her own spit. She convulsed, and all I could do was hold her and pray that the paramedics would get there fast.

Chapter 40

The cops arrived seconds behind the paramedics. The EMTs asked me a slew of questions, and I told them what I knew. They could put the rest together with the bottle of pills. They were pressing on her chest the whole way out to the ambulance.

Then the cops got their hands on me.

"Hey, you're that Greco kid, aren't you?" one of the cops asked.

"Yes, sir," I said.

"Right," his partner said. "You've got a little brother? Tommy Troublemaker."

"Yes, sir," I said, not caring they knew who my younger brother was. They sat me down mere feet from where I'd found Mrs. Mockingham and only inches from where the pills still laid.

"Looks like somebody broke in," one of the cops said. "Was that you?"

"Yes, sir," I answered.

"Why did you break in?" the other cop asked.

The story came quickly. "I'm only in town for the week. I was coming to wish Mrs. Mockingham a happy Thanksgiving."

"And you thought you would bust in the front door and . . ."

"No, sir," I said. "I called ahead of time. She said she was home. When I got here, and she didn't answer, I got worried. And then I looked through the window and saw her on the floor, so . . ."

"So you busted in the front door. How convenient. Weird, she told you to come over, then pops a fistful of pills." This was the other cop; apparently, they weren't playing good cop, bad cop. They were both playing the bad cop role. Lucky me.

"How exactly do you know Mrs. Mockingham?" he asked.

"She's a friend of the family. We've known her for a long time. You can ask my mom."

"We will," one of them said, making a note in his little book. "You're the one that called 911?" he asked.

"Yes, sir. As soon as I found her."

"Why didn't you do CPR?" the other one asked.

"I don't know how. I'm sorry, should I have—"

One of the cops held his hand up. "That's all right, kid. Do you remember me?"

I stared at him. "No, sir."

"I was a friend of your pops. We went to high school together. We both played outfield. I remember you. You were the good kid, weren't you?"

I nodded, but didn't want to admit that I was the good one and Tommy was the bad one. He was still my little brother. There's loyalty among family.

"We don't want to keep you. I bet you need to get back to school, right?"

"Yes, sir," I said.

"You think you guys will make it to a bowl game?"

Things had already switched to what they were really interested in. They didn't care about the poor woman who'd tried to kill herself and was on her way to the hospital. She was most likely already dead. How many times did they see these kinds of scenes? Neither man looked particularly disturbed.

"I think we've got a good shot, sir." I didn't have to act nervous. I was nervous.

"You think we should put money on the game?" the guy asked his partner.

The partner looked me up and down. "I don't know. Kid, what do you think?"

When I didn't answer, they looked at each other again and laughed.

"Don't answer that. We don't want anybody to think that you gave us an inside tip." The man who had known my father gave me a wink as if he knew everything about my life.

"Officers, do I have to go down to the station with you? My family . . ."

"Don't worry about it, kid. Tell you what, run through it again. Tell us what happened. We'll take down your statement and then head to the hospital to see how Mrs."—he looked down at his pad—"Mrs. Mockingham is doing."

I told him my story, exactly the way I had told him before. I hoped I didn't miss any details. I mentioned the phone call. Of course, I didn't mention what the phone call was about. I didn't think they had Mrs. Mockingham's line tapped. I explained all the way up through calling 911 and waiting for the paramedics.

"And that's it. Then you got here," I said.

They each made a couple more notes, closed their notebooks, and put them back in their pockets. The whole routine felt rehearsed. My dad's old friend stood and shook my hand. "It's good to see you, Greco. Keep up the good work at school."

"Yes, sir," I said. Another crew had arrived and was taping off the scene. Hopefully there was no crime here as far as the cops were concerned. The last thing I needed was to be labeled the Old-Lady Killer.

"Come on, I'll make sure nobody gives you a hard time," the cop said while holding the police tape up so I could duck under. I was about to walk away when he asked, "Hey, kid?"

I turned.

"You by any chance know where Mr. Mockingham is?"

"No, sir," I said. I guess I had assumed that he had passed away, but I didn't say that.

"You didn't know that he's disappeared?"

"Disappeared?" I asked.

The cops shared another look. "If you hear anything about Mr. Mockingham, you let us know, kid, you hear?"

"Yes, sir," I said. When I walked away, I couldn't help but wonder what the hell was really going on.

Chapter 41

As I walked home, I tried to put it all together. The missing ledger. Mrs. Mockingham on "vacation." Her husband missing. Visions of her lying on the ground, the pill bottle in her hand.

I thought about going to the hospital to see if she was going to be okay. If she was awake, maybe she would talk to me. Then again, if my visit had triggered her to try to take her own life, what the hell would my visit to the hospital do?

That's when it hit me. If she did wake up and she did talk to the cops, what would she tell them? Shit, I didn't have much time. My walk went to a jog and then a run. Maybe in my next life I'll learn to hitchhike. When I got home, Mom was eating leftover Chinese in the living room. There was rice all over the floor.

"There's my baby boy," she said. An empty bottle of Carlo Rossi sat precariously on the edge of the table.

"Geez, Mom, it's not even twelve o'clock."

"What? I was hungry," she said, slurring. The top she was wearing was too tight for her figure, and she was threatening to spill out of the damn thing.

"Where's Tommy?" I asked.

"I don't know, probably in his room." I went to his room, and of course he wasn't there. I walked back and turned off the television.

"Hey, what are you doing? I was watching that," she said.

"Mom, listen to me. You know Mrs. Mockingham at the bank, right?"

"Yeah, sure. We used to teach Sunday school together."

I'd forgotten about that fact.

"Do you know what happened to her husband?"

"Her husband?" she asked stupidly.

"Yes, Mom, her husband. What happened to Mr. Mockingham?"

It took a few seconds for her brain to process.

"I think I heard something about him. Maybe he left or retired."

"He disappeared, Mom. Now what did you hear?"

"Probably good riddance, if you ask me," she said. "He was always looking down my dress. Never paid two hoots to his wife. Poor woman. Though I make much better brownies than her."

"Focus, Mom," I said.

"Michael, what is wrong with you? You know you can't talk to me that way."

"Mom, Mrs. Mockingham is in the hospital. She tried to kill herself."

"What? Now you're pulling my leg. Come on, turn the television back on. I was in the middle of a show."

If I was another man, I might have slapped my own mother.

"Mom, listen. I need you to focus."

"Fine," she said, grabbing the next bottle of Carlo Rossi and twisting off the top. "Do you want some?" she asked, giggling.

"Mom, what did you hear about Mr. Mockingham?"

She licked her lips and gazed lovingly at the bottle in her hands.

"I think I heard somebody, maybe at the liquor store, maybe at the grocery. I don't know. They were talking about it. I think they said that Judy had been crying at the bank. I'm not sure, I can't remember. You know my memory."

Of course I knew her memory, especially when she was drinking. I tried to tone down my voice. In those moments when she was on her way to blackout, it was like soothing a patient into a hypnotic trance. I sat down next to her. I held her hand. That got her attention. She nearly swooned with motherly love.

"Oh, Michael, have I told you how handsome you are? My baby boy's all grown up." I let her tuck my long hair behind my ear.

"Mom?"

"Yes, honey."

"What else did you hear about Mr. Mockingham?"

"You know how that goes. There's all sorts of rumors. Some people said that Judy kicked him out. Others say that he ran away with another woman. Probably that hoochie who works at the salon. She never could get my hair right."

"What do *you* think, Mom?"

"I think they're all wrong. The Mockinghams, they're one of those kinds of couples."

"What kinds of couples, Mom?"

"The kind that'll never leave each other, like your grandparents. They hated each other, you know? But your grandmother would never leave because she was Catholic. Your grandfather would never leave because he didn't want anybody to look at him like he wasn't a good husband. Therefore, they stayed together, miserable. But together."

"Are you saying the Mockinghams were miserable?" I asked.

"I'm giving you an example. The Mockinghams were cordial. Yes, I think that's the word, isn't it?"

I nodded.

"I don't think Mr. Mockingham would've run away with a girl. I can't imagine anyone taking him."

"Do you think Mrs. Mockingham would kick him out of the house?"

"Are you kidding? And shake herself off the top of the ladder at the church? You know what those women would do to her?"

I did. I'd seen it happen. Despite the high level of impropriety in my hometown, divorce was uncommon. Death was the more likely cause of marital splits.

"I hope something hasn't happened to him," she said, like she really cared.

"Me, too, Mom. Listen, if you hear anything else, can you tell me, please?"

"Of course, honey. I didn't know you cared so much about the Mockinghams."

I cared more about the ledger at that moment than Mrs. Mockingham, but yes, I did feel bad about her. That's when Mom snapped her fingers and said, "I remember now."

"What's that, Mom?"

She closed her eyes and put her index finger in the air.

"Yes, I know who told me about Mr. Mockingham." Her eyes opened and drifted away from me over to the kitchen. "There he is right there. Your uncle Freddy was the one who told me."

I turned and saw Uncle Freddy standing in the middle of the kitchen. How had I not heard him come in? He had his arms crossed over his chest and was glaring at me.

Chapter 42

"Freddy, tell Michael what you told me."

Uncle Freddy stood there glaring. "I need a word with your son," he said finally.

"But we were having such a great time." Mom patted me on the hand like we were best friends again. Had we ever been best friends?

"It's okay, Mom," I said, not taking my eyes from my uncle.

"Well, okay. You men do your business, and then come sit with me, watch my show, have some wine, and this Chinese food is still delicious."

She was still babbling on when we left the kitchen and walked outside.

"I heard you got in trouble," Uncle Freddy said.

"I didn't get in trouble," I said.

"No? What do you call it when the cops are about to put you in cuffs?"

I held up my hands. "No handcuffs, see?"

"Don't be a smart-ass with me, boy."

"You are not my dad, so you can go screw yourself."

That got his attention. The veins on his fat neck stood out, and his face went red. "There's going to come a time when you're no longer welcome here," he said.

"This is *my* home," I said.

"Not for long."

"And what's that supposed to mean?"

He gave me a thin smile. "I think you'll see."

He went to pat me on the arm, and I slapped his hand away. Uncle Freddy shrugged and walked by me and went back into the house. But before he closed the door behind him, he said, "Too bad about the Mockinghams. They should have listened when they had a chance."

Chapter 43

I didn't want to go back inside, so I drove Mom's car to the hospital instead. At first, they passed me around and didn't want to tell me where Mrs. Mockingham was. I fully expected someone to say *You better visit the morgue,* but no one did.

Then a nice nurse, who looked younger than me, said, "She just woke up. I can take you to her if you like."

I'm not embarrassed to say that I put on all my charms to get through her honest probing.

Mrs. Mockingham was sitting up in bed, pale, and scooping out canned fruit with a plastic spoon.

"Here you go," the nice nurse said, ushering me into the room and then closing the door behind me.

If it were possible, I'm pretty sure Mrs. Mockingham's face went even more pale. "Greco, you shouldn't be here," she said. She spilled her canned fruit all over her tray.

I went to the bed and helped her clean it up.

"How are you feeling?" I asked.

"Better," she said, but she kept scooting farther away from me and acted like my touch would give her a disease.

"That was pretty scary," I said.

"Scary?" she asked.

"Yes, ma'am. Didn't they tell you?"

"Tell me what?"

"I was the one who found you. I was the one who called 911."

She shook her head and started crying. "Oh God, no. I'm so sorry. I didn't mean for anyone to . . ."

I took one of her hands. It was cold and shivering. "Mrs. Mockingham, it's okay. It's not your fault, and I'm fine. I promise."

I let her cry and just sat there, letting the emotions ooze from her every pore. The crying turned to sobbing and then back to normal crying again.

"I kept dreaming about you, and I couldn't figure out why. The police came by, but the nurses were nice enough to say that I didn't want to talk to anyone. I lied to them. I lied, and I said that I accidentally took too many pills, but I'm pretty sure they don't believe me."

Of course they don't believe you, I thought, but that's not what I said. "It's okay," I said. "It was an accident. Though I think I might have to pay for your front door."

"My front door?" Mrs. Mockingham asked, sniffling.

"I had to bust it in to get inside."

"You did?" she asked.

"Yes, ma'am. Just like in the movies. Felt like Magnum, P.I."

She sniffled again, and I handed her a tissue. "I'm so sorry, Greco. I'm sorry you have to see me like this. I'm sorry you had to see me like that. I can't imagine. You'll probably have nightmares."

I could have told her that my regular nightmares were way worse than seeing an old lady on the ground with a bottle of pills, but I didn't. I needed her to keep talking.

"Has Mr. Mockingham been by?"

Fresh tears sprang to her eyes, but she didn't sob. She shook her head instead.

"Where is Mr. Mockingham?" I asked.

Her lips quivered, and I thought she was going to start sobbing again. If she did, I might have had to call for the nurse. She looked so weak and fragile.

"I can't talk about it," she said.

Greco

I needed her to talk about it, so I pressed. "I can help you. I really can," I said. "And Mr. Mockingham, him too."

She shook her head. "It's too late for him." She dabbed at her nose with the Kleenex. I grabbed her another.

"What happened to Mr. Mockingham?"

She kept shaking her head. "It's my fault. It's all my fault."

This wasn't getting anywhere. At any moment, the nurse would come back in and tell me it was time to leave. I tried something else.

"Mrs. Mockingham, did you let someone else in to my safe-deposit box?"

That got her attention. That made her perk up. I saw her professionalism then. Years of working at a bank couldn't be snapped out by grief.

"They said they were going to hurt me," she said, but her voice was stronger now.

"Who said they were going to hurt you?" I asked.

She didn't answer that question. Instead she said, "I told my husband about it. I suppose it's okay to tell you that we've been sleeping in separate rooms for years. That can probably tell you what our relationship was like. He went to work; I went to work. We came home. We had separate dinners. I would leave before him, and we didn't have to talk much. It was a good arrangement, but when I told him what happened, he became my old Brady again. He was a strong man, a handsome man. He worked construction for thirty-three years. His hands could crush a full beer can." Mrs. Mockingham's eyes drifted to the window. "He held me for the first time in years," she said. "He said he would protect me. He said everything was going to be okay. That night, we slept in the same bed, and he held me."

Big tears were running down her face, the tears of lost love.

She turned back to me and wiped the tears from her face. "Brady and I were married when I was twenty. He moved me here right after our honeymoon. It wasn't much, a couple days down at the beach. We made a home, and we tried to have kids, but we couldn't, so Brady

155

suggested that I get a job, and though I wasn't qualified, I started as a cashier at the grocery store. Then I got lucky and overheard someone say that they were hiring at the bank for a new teller. I applied, and, knowing what I know now, I can't believe they hired me. They took a chance. I was a hard worker, a fast learner, and since the age of twenty-four, I've been at the same bank, and never once in all those years have I done anything illegal. Sure, I've made mistakes. We all have. And yes, I know what goes on in this town. This town used to have so much promise. I know that not all the money the bank has is clean money, but that's not my problem. I do my job. I keep my nose clean. I live my life. I teach Sunday school. I go to church and . . ."

"You're a good woman," I said. "Nobody denies that, Mrs. Mockingham."

She nodded. "I appreciate you saying that, Greco. It means a lot coming from you." She grabbed hold of my hand tightly. "I want you to make me a promise. When all this is done, you go back to that school of yours, and you never come back. Do you understand me?"

I nodded. She glanced back at the window for a second and then back to me.

"When they threatened me, I should have gone to the police, but I didn't take it seriously. Brady paid the price, God rest his soul. They showed me Polaroid pictures and said I'd end up the same way. And now I've been given a second chance. You saved my life, Greco, and for that I will always be grateful. I'll light a candle for you every Sunday, I promise. In a moment of weakness, God showed me his strength."

The tears were gone now, and I saw the toughness in her.

"I'm so sorry, Greco. I don't like to be the one to tell you this." There was strength mixed with deep sorrow when she told me the punch line. "It was your brother, Tommy, who I let in to see your safe-deposit box."

Chapter 44

I can't tell you what I felt when I left the hospital. Anger. Sadness. Despair. Mrs. Mockingham's revelation that Tommy had been the one to take the ledger floored me. I'd expected her to confirm my suspicions that Uncle Freddy was the culprit, but it had been my own brother.

That's when so many things made sense. I'd barely seen Tommy since being home. He was always gone or locked in his room. I could only assume that he had fallen in with the wrong crowd. But had he fallen in with the toughest crowd, Johnny Cheese and his men; he was part of the same thing. The underground workings of an ancient system.

It happens every day and all around the world. You can't get a loan from the bank. You find another way to get the money, usually at a very high interest rate; those loans are made, and the world continues to go around.

Or maybe you want to build a porch in your backyard and the city's giving you a hard time, so you grease the wheels with a little bit of cash. That's the type of town my father liked to tread in, the type I escaped. And now I'd gotten sucked back in.

But Tommy? How could I have been so stupid? How could I have missed the signs?

I didn't want to go home, but I went there. I walked around the side of the house to Tommy's bedroom window and peeked in. He wasn't there. I went and looked in the other windows. I didn't see Tommy, but I did see Uncle Freddy and my mom making out on the couch. Definitely not going in there.

I took Mom's car again and started making rounds in town at the neighbors, and at Tommy's friends' houses. No one had seen Tommy. I made a guess. Where would I have gone? Where did I go on those lonely days when I wanted to be away? The football stadium.

That's where I found Tommy, sitting at the fifty yard line, smoking a cigarette. "You found me," he said.

I don't know what kept me from tackling him right then and there and beating the story out of him. The truth was, he was still my little brother. And though he tried to look tough with a cigarette dangling out of his mouth, he was still a kid, a kid growing into a man, a stupid, stupid man like our father. Sadness overtook me, and I almost didn't want to ask Tommy about the ledger. I didn't want to ask him about any of it. I wanted to say goodbye and leave. How many times have I said now that I wanted to fly away, that I wanted to fade into the world and never see my old life again?

"Got anymore?" I asked. He pulled out a pack and handed me one. I took his cigarette and lit mine.

"Some Thanksgiving, huh?" he said.

"Yeah, I'm surprised they don't call us the Brady Bunch," I said.

Tommy grunted. "I think I would've gotten in a hell of a lot of trouble if Marcia Brady was my stepsister," he said.

We sat there for a while, two brothers smoking cigarettes. Funny enough, I'd look back on this moment years later as one of my fondest memories. You could tell it was getting ready to snow, because it was so quiet. The clouds puffed overhead; the cold wrapped us and tickled our skin. In subsequent years, when I would go through something hard and seemingly insurmountable, I would find a high school football field and go sit at the fifty yard line.

I don't pull out cigarettes anymore, but sometimes I'll take a cigar and remember that day with Tommy. Because in some way, we felt like we were cocooned in our own little world away from it all. And when I closed my eyes, I imagined a new world, a better world. A world where Tommy and I were friends. Where Mom was sober and we moved away, far away. Maybe Tommy and I would start a business together. Maybe Mom would be our secretary. She loved talking on the phone.

That's where my mind went as I sat there that day. My heart at peace for the first time in days, it was Tommy who broke the silence.

"I'm sorry, Mikey," he said.

"For what?" I asked.

"For being a shit. For ditching class, for not listening to my coach, for not doing everything you said to do."

"I didn't say you had to be perfect," I said.

"Yeah, but . . . oh hell. Mom's always talking about you, you know. Her beautiful boy, how proud she is of you. And then she looks at me and says that I'm going to turn out like Dad. And it's not a compliment. She talks about him a lot, especially when she's drinking. At least when Uncle Freddy's not around. She says what a fuckup he was. That he slept around for years, that he liked to pretend that none of it happened. Then she'd point out that I do the same damn thing, that I'm always making excuses, and you know what? I'm starting to believe it, Mikey. I'm starting to believe that I'm just like Dad, that I'm going to die early too. That the world is giving me the hand that I deserve."

"Don't say that," I said. "You can make whatever life you want."

"That's bullshit, and you know it," he said. "Look at you. You shouldn't be here right now. If I was you, I'd never come back to this fucking place." He flicked the butt of his cigarette away. "I thought about leaving, taking the money I have, hopping on a bus, and going far away. Maybe I'll enlist in the army, who knows? Maybe the navy will take me."

"You're too young," I said.

"People have lied before. I read this story about a guy who enlisted when he was thirteen in World War Two. I'm sure I can find somebody who can forge some documents for me. Besides, do I look fifteen?"

I'm not sure if it was for the first time, but I really looked at him then, and he did not look fifteen. He looked like he was eighteen. He didn't look like me, but he sure as hell looked like Dad. I wondered if every morning when Tommy went to the bathroom, did he look in the mirror and say *There's Dad. I'm just like him.*

"Listen to me, Tommy. You can be whatever you want to be."

"You sound like a fucking army commercial," he said. "Is that my answer, go enlist?"

"There are worse things," I said.

"Sure, sure. But not college, right? I'm too stupid to go to college."

"I never said that."

"Yeah, but you sure as hell thought it, didn't you? You've never given me a fair shake. You've always thought I was a fuckup. If I wanted to hang out with you, you pushed me away, you said I was too young, too immature, too much of a little shit."

I was embarrassed to admit that I had done those things, but when there's a four-year age gap between you and your sibling—hell, even a one-year gap—at that point in your life, do you really want your little brother chasing you around when you're trying to get a scholarship, get good grades, and date a girl? The answer is no.

"I'm sorry, Tommy. I didn't know. Hell, I guess what I'm trying to say is I'm a stupid fucking kid too."

Tommy exhaled. "Look at us, two stupid kids sitting out in the cold. What would Dad say?"

"He'd say we're family. He'd say we should stick together. And I would hope he would say we need to tell each other the truth. So, here's the truth, Tommy. I'm scared there's something going on here that I haven't been able to piece together," I lied. "And I need your help. I need you to tell me the truth, because if we're brothers, you owe me that. Hell, tell me because of all the breakfasts I made for you. Don't forget about the dinners too."

Tommy stared at the ground.

Greco

"I need you to level with me, Tommy. You need to tell me what's been going on." Tommy kept his eyes locked on the ground. I assumed he was going to run from yet another problem. He'd gotten used to it, like Dad, but he didn't get up and walk away. He looked at me straight in the eyes and said, "I took the book, Mikey. I went to the bank, and they let me in."

"And who told you to do that, Tommy? Was it Johnny Cheese?"

Tommy shook his head, long and slow. "It was Uncle Freddy. He said if I didn't do it, he was going to kill me and put Mom in a mental institution."

Chapter 45

Tommy and I sat there for a long time. I was sad and disappointed, feeling that everything I'd done up until that point to help Tommy and show him there was a better way had been a complete and utter failure. Then I asked myself, Was it really his fault? Sure, I'd been lucky enough to get away, but had I really? Look at where I was now, back home dealing with the same shit I always dealt with—family. And what a crooked mess it was. Less than a day before, I had to stand face to face with Mr. Romano, and what the hell was I going to do now?

"You haven't asked me why," Tommy said.

"Why what?" I asked.

"Why I did it; why I helped Uncle Freddy."

"You already told me. I don't really care anymore," I said.

You know when you hit that point of complete exhaustion with your emotions? I'd hit that point. I wanted to lie down, close my eyes, and sleep for a very long time.

Snow was falling now, and I looked up into the sky, wishing that the billowing clouds would take me away. Tommy nudged me.

"Hey, I said, you didn't ask why."

"And I said, I don't care."

"Mikey, look at me."

I ripped my gaze from the clouds and looked at my little brother. God, he looked like Dad in his prime. Dad untainted by the world, at least in my eyes. Dad so young and full of life, and now he was dead and buried and gone forever. "Okay, Tommy, tell me why."

The words came out like he'd been saving it for months. "He said he was going to kill Mom; he said he was going to kill you, and then he was going to blame it all on me."

"I don't believe you," I said.

"What do you mean you don't believe me? You think I'm lying?"

I was too exhausted to argue. If the world was going to snap shut the final chapter of my life, I was done fighting.

"Uncle Freddy's all talk," I said, "and you believed him. And besides, this life, this place, has a way of sucking you in and never letting you go. I tried to tell you that, but look at you. Like Dad, you're waist deep in quicksand, and you don't know it."

"You don't think I know it?" There were tears in his eyes now, but I didn't care. "This wasn't some bullshit. He was serious. He told me exactly how he was going to do it."

"Okay, Tommy. Whatever you say. First you tell me that he's going to put her in a mental institution; now you're saying that he was going to kill her. And here I thought Disney had the monopoly on tall tales."

I got to my feet wearily and started to walk away, but Tommy pushed me from behind. That got my blood flowing. "What the hell was that?" I asked.

"You need to listen to me."

"I have listened to you, Tommy. I've listened to your excuses, your reasons. I've listened to everything you've said, because don't forget, I'm the one that raised you—not Mom, not Dad—me. I'm tired of listening to you, because quite frankly, I don't believe you anymore."

He pushed me again, but I dug in and pushed him back. When he came back at me, he was swinging. Compared to the swipes I'd taken on the football field, his swing felt lazy, and I easily ducked under and tackled him full on. We grappled on the ground for a minute, but I quickly got the upper hand, putting him in a chokehold, thinking that Tommy would tap out, give up. But he kept fighting, kept trying to twist away. He elbowed me in the ribs. I held on for dear life, and then for some reason, and I don't know why, I let him go. I pushed him off me and got to my feet. He was gagging from where I choked him and looked up at me through tear-filled eyes.

"I'm not lying," he said. He was eight years old all over again. He'd stolen a package of OREOs from the grocery store, and I'd caught him eating them in his room. When I'd taken him back to the grocery store, half-eaten OREOs and all, to confront the manager, to make him pay back what he'd stolen, a nervous cashier had been the one to walk into the manager's office to tell us that she'd bought the OREOs for the poor kid who looked half-starved. Tommy hadn't stolen the OREOs; not that he didn't steal other things later, but that time it wasn't his fault. Somebody had taken pity on him. He told the truth, but did I apologize?

Of course not. I'm me.

At eleven, going on twelve, I was the man of the house when Dad chose to disappear. I was embarrassed and dragged him out of the store, but I'll never forget the look in his eyes. It was the same look that he was giving me now. He was telling the truth. I was going to reach down to help him up, to tell him I was sorry, to tell him I believed him, but the piercing screech of sirens filled the air, and for some reason, some connection, I knew what that meant, and so did Tommy. We didn't say a word; we just ran as fast as we could to the car and sped home.

Chapter 46

We got to the house as the firefighters were hooking up their hoses to the fire hydrant across the street. Our house was shooting flames from the roof. Black smoke billowed from the windows.

"You stay here," I told Tommy.

"No way. I'm going with you," he said.

We slipped past the group of firefighters who were getting ready to go in.

"Hey, kids, you can't go in there!" one of the firefighters shouted, but it was too late. We burst in the front door and were immediately greeted by immense heat. We dropped to the ground and crawled forward. I could hear the firefighters yelling behind us, but there wasn't a damn thing they could do to pull me out.

First, we went to the living room, which was, surprisingly, still untouched by flames. The kitchen was cooking like a campfire; it was probably the source of everything. Tommy and I had both tucked our faces into our shirts. We crouched and clawed our way forward. My eyes burned from the smoke, and my skin prickled from the heat.

"The bedroom!" I yelled.

We moved that way, but one of the walls caved in, and we had to roll to the side quickly to get out of its way. Part of the wall caught Tommy on the leg, and he screamed. I pulled him away.

"You okay?" I asked.

"I'm okay."

We were going to crawl forward again when a firefighter appeared through the smoke and grabbed Tommy.

"No!" I heard him yell, but at least he would be safe. I let them take him. I had to find Mom. By now, it was getting blazing hot at the floor, so I crept in a crouch around flames as my hair singed, and I struggled to breathe.

A little farther, I told myself.

I heard a sound like a deep yawning and looked up to see the ceiling break apart. Instead of creeping, I bolted the last few feet just in time as the roof caved in. Mom's door was closed, and I felt it for heat.

No heat, thank God. The door was locked, so I had to put my shoulder to it. Seemed to be I was getting good at busting down doors.

Mom was lying on the bed, a liquor bottle still in her hand. There was a bottle of pills on the bedside table, and for a split second, I thought that she'd gone the way of Mrs. Mockingham. But when I felt for a pulse, it was still there. She was passed-out drunk. Even though I'd closed the door, flames were already licking through where I busted the doorjamb. There was only one way to go—through the window.

But the window was small, and at about shoulder height. I was strong, but not strong enough to pull myself and Mom through it. In fact, when I tried to open the window, it wouldn't budge. They'd later tell me that someone had glued the window shut. I looked all around for something, anything to help me open it. There was a small metal stool that my mother used to sit on in front of a mirror to put on her makeup. I picked it up and didn't hesitate before smashing it into the window. Oxygen poured in, feeding the flames, and like a many-tentacled beast, the flames from the door reached out toward the bed.

I cleaned the glass around the edges of the window as much as I could with the stool. Then I screamed out the window, "Over here, the back of the house!" hoping that someone would hear me. I picked my mom up and took her to the window. Still, nobody was there. There was only one thing to do. I dropped her as gently as I could. She landed heavily. I climbed out the window as carefully as I could, but I still got cuts all on my forearms. I didn't feel the pain.

I picked up Mom and jogged around the house to where an ambulance now sat waiting. Nobody told me I was a stupid kid. Nobody told me I was a hero either.

They took my mother from my arms and sat me down on the back of the ambulance. Someone put an oxygen mask on my face, and sweet, sweet air filled my lungs. I kept coughing, and my eyes still burned.

"I'll get some water to rinse your eyes," a paramedic said, though my eyes were so blurry that I couldn't see what she looked like.

"Where's my brother?" I asked through the mask.

"They've taken him to the hospital, son."

It was one of the firefighters. The rest were dousing the house with their high-pressured hoses. When my eyes cleared, I could see that there was a crowd of neighbors gathering.

Curious onlookers probably thought that the Grecos had finally done it. They'd finally burned their lives to the ground. I avoided their gazes because I really didn't care.

Another paramedic appeared and said, "We're taking your mother to the hospital. You can get in the ambulance if you'd like, or you can wait here. There's another ambulance coming."

For some reason, all I could think about was how expensive three ambulances would be.

"I'm fine," I said, taking off the oxygen mask. I felt like I'd smoked four packs of cigarettes. But other than that, I felt okay.

"Listen, smoke inhalation is no joke, kid," the paramedic said. "You need to get checked out."

"Sure," I said, "but there's something I need to get before I go. It's at my neighbor's house." I lied.

She looked at me dubiously but nodded. "If you're not back in two minutes, I'm coming to find you," she said.

I smiled and promised I'd be back in two minutes. But I wasn't going to my neighbor's house. I did walk down the street. I took a left and made a show of going toward the Androwskys' front door.

When I glanced back to see if anybody was looking, nobody was, so I ducked around the side of the house and rested my back against the cool wall. My lungs were burning. It was hard to catch my breath. I closed my eyes and willed my heart to slow. I should have gone to the hospital with the ambulance. Tommy was safe, and now Mom was safe, and I had to keep them that way. What I needed was space, time to think. What was the next move? Going to the hospital meant surrendering to house arrest. I didn't think Mr. Romano would give me a pass just because I'd sucked down some smoke. Think, Greco, think!

When I opened my eyes, for a second I thought I was hallucinating. But there was Uncle Freddy standing in front of me.

"Lookee what I found," he said. "You're just like your daddy, sticking your nose where it doesn't belong. I knew that fire would bring the hero running."

Before I could react, his hand, which had been at his side and was holding a baseball bat, swung hard, hitting me in the side of the head. Whether it was because of my genetic predisposition to withstand hits to the head or the fact that I was young and strong, I didn't immediately go out. I did go to the ground. My senses swooned. And when I looked up through the narrowing lens that was my eyesight, I saw Uncle Freddy standing over me, and I thought I heard him say, "Another great Greco bites the dust."

Chapter 47

My head felt like it had been caved in by a cudgel. My vision spun. I vomited. When I tried to lean forward, I realized that my hands were tied behind me.

I felt a little bit better after emptying the contents of my stomach, but when I looked around, the dark room that I was in didn't make me feel much better. Slowly, the pieces of my recent memory came back together. Tommy at the fifty yard line, the earsplitting sirens of the fire trucks, going in to get Mom, the fire. So much fire. And then Uncle Freddy. Once again, he was one step ahead. He'd started the fire. He'd baited us home.

"How do you feel?" came a voice from the dark.

"Like shit," I said. "How about you, Uncle Freddy? How's it feel to take down your own family?"

He appeared from the darkness, a bottle of cheap beer in his hand.

"Let's get something straight. You are not my family." He poked me in the chest with the bottle. "You're my brother's family, and I disowned him a long time ago."

"Why?" I croaked through a coughing fit.

"He was just like you, Greco. Too good for his little brother. He always looked down on me. Always said I'd amount to nothing. Well, lookee who's still alive and kicking."

He spread his arms wide as if his life were something to brag about.

"You're a real pain in my ass, kid. Same as your dad."

"My dad was never home," I said. "My dad didn't care about us."

Uncle Freddy laughed. "So, you don't know," he said.

"Know what?" I asked.

He was laughing hard now. "This is good. Really good," he said. "I thought for sure that you knew, but I guess I shouldn't be surprised, when I found out that your mom didn't know." He laughed. It echoed in the dark room. What the hell was he talking about? Like his laugh had been cut off with an emergency valve, he stopped abruptly and stared at me.

"You and your dad, you always walked so righteous, like you were untouchable. But who's untouchable now?"

There was a gleam in his eye that promised nothing but pain. But I was past caring. I wanted to know what the hell he was talking about. I didn't have to ask. He leaned down, close, but not too close. He whispered toward my ear.

And what he said filled me with more despair and loss than I'd ever felt. And when my head slumped to my chest and Uncle Freddy laughed again, I could imagine that I would feel more pain soon. Much, much more pain.

Chapter 48

I don't know how long my uncle left me tied up there. I wallowed in my self-pity. I thought back to when Dad was alive, if there had been signs, if what Uncle Freddy said was true. But why would he lie?

Little memories cropped up, things that I hadn't thought about in a decade. Dad taking me to a Bulls game to see the rookie Michael Jordan revolutionize the NBA. He'd left me at our seats, not bad seats but not great. He told me he was going to buy me a hot dog and a soda. Told me not to move, but there was a creepy guy a couple of rows over who kept giving me the stink eye. I got nervous and went looking for Dad. I found him not holding a hot dog and a soda but talking to a guy outside the bathroom. A guy I had never seen. A guy who looked like he was trying too hard to fit in. Even at that age, I felt the weirdness of the scene.

"Your father was an FBI informant," Uncle Freddy had said in my ear. "He was a snitch."

Snitch.

My father was a snitch.

A four-letter word where I'm from.

Is that why he'd been gone so many times? He always said he was putting some deals together, some this or that, a sales gig. Sometimes he called it networking before networking was a term used in popular lingo.

"Your father was an FBI informant."

Those words kept rolling around in my head, but I hadn't seen anything in the ledger to prove that. I thought about it, imagining the details in my head. Not a soul had breathed anything about this new truth to me. My heart thudded when I thought about Johnny Cheese. Did he know? Is that what he thought was in the ledger? Why hadn't he and his men escorted me to the bank and taken it?

I didn't know.

A dull ache spread through me, an ache of regret. What if Dad had told me? What if he'd tried to tell me? What if I hadn't spent years hating him for being gone? But would this have changed anything? I was far from a perfect kid, a knucklehead, some would say. But had Dad made me that way? Had he toughened me up, prepared me for the future by being away, making me the man of the house? At what price? I would give everything up—and I do mean everything—to have him back, to ask him the truth.

It was dawning on me as I sat there, not really feeling the pain in my body, that it was the truth. That there was evidence scattered in my path. I didn't really want to see it. My adolescent and teenage vision was too shadowed by embarrassment that we didn't have enough food to eat, embarrassment that I had to take care of my family, embarrassment that my dad was never around.

A door creaked open, and Uncle Freddy strolled in, all fat-cat happy. "You still feeling sorry for yourself?" he asked.

In response, I spat at his feet. He smacked me across the face. It stung, but it didn't really hurt.

"Is that all you've got?" I asked through gritted teeth.

He looked down at me, surprised, but not for long. The next hit was a closed fist, and that hurt. This time when I spat at his feet, it was blood.

"I'd take you through a couple rounds if I had the time," Uncle Freddy said, rubbing his fist in his opposite palm. "You going to come quietly, or do I need to tie you up and throw you in the trunk?"

"Where are we going?" I asked.

"Back to school, smart guy."

That got my attention.

"I'm not going with you," I said.

"The hell you aren't." He grabbed me by the hair and yanked me to my feet, chair and all. "Now listen here, you little shit, time's ticking, and if you don't do as I say, I'll finish the deal with your mother, then I'll take care of Tommy." He leaned in real close, almost so close that our noses were touching. "And the next person we'll visit is your girlfriend, the pretty one from New York."

"You stay away from her," I screamed, lunging and then trying to bite him, headbutt him, kick him, anything. But he held me back, and with my arms tied around the back of me and bound to a chair, I was useless. I thrashed around, and he laughed in my face.

"There you go. There's the spark you're going to need," he said. "Now sit down and shut up. I'm going to untie you from the chair, but if you try to do anything . . ." He pulled a pistol from his waistband. "I may not be a good shot at twenty yards, but I sure as hell am a good shot at point-blank range." He put the barrel to my temple, and I saw in his eyes that he meant it.

I didn't move as he unbound my hands from the chair, let me get to my feet, and then retied my hands again behind my back.

I figured I didn't have much to lose. All I had to do was wait for my opening, and for now, I would go along like a compliant little boy.

Chapter 49

When we got upstairs, there was a room full of Uncle Freddy's cronies lounging about.

"Get your feet off the coffee table," Uncle Freddy barked.

His cronies complied slowly. I counted them. Six, not including Freddy. So much for my thoughts of getaway.

"Hey, isn't that the kid from the paper?" one of the cronies said.

"Shut your mouth," Uncle Freddy said. "Pack up your shit. We're leaving."

"What? The game is starting."

"I said, pack up your shit, and let's go."

The cronies moved more than a little reluctantly. Looked like Uncle Freddy was far from Napoleon, though he barked like Patton. It seemed that he was the only one who was armed. At least half had to polish off beers before leaving.

Uncle Freddy was antsy and kept snapping little commands like "Pick up your feet. Stop complaining."

He gave me to a crony with a huge, greasy forehead. The man stared at me. Uncle Freddy talked to the others in the front room.

When the men reappeared, Uncle Freddy said, "We take three cars. Don't speed."

"Oh, come on. It's a Saturday night," one of them said.

"I said, don't speed."

Uncle Freddy was really on edge now. What I wanted to do was push him over that edge.

"Yeah, Uncle Freddy, why don't we do a little drag racing?" I asked.

He ignored me. At least I'd tried. He marched me out the front door, and we were piling into three cars when headlights blared in, four trucks skidding to the curb.

"What the fuck?" Uncle Freddy murmured.

At first I thought it was the cops, then I thought it was Johnny Cheese, but it was neither.

"Let him go" came a voice.

It was Tommy. What the hell?

"Go home, kid," Uncle Freddy said.

And then another familiar voice. "He said, let him go."

My roommate, Leroy, walked into view, followed by Wilbur Downs and most of the offensive line. Pip Harrington was there, grinning like this was a game, as were some of the others; there were eleven in all, including Tommy and Leroy.

"Who the hell do you think you are?" Uncle Freddy asked.

Leroy looked at Wilbur, and Wilbur grinned. With a roar, he and the rest of the offensive line tore into the shocked cronies. Middle-aged girth was no match for the ferocity of NCAA football. Heads bashed against cars. Men screamed as collarbones were snapped, legs were broken.

I felt Uncle Freddy let me go, and I saw why. Leroy was laying in at full speed. Uncle Freddy spread his arms wide to catch him, but Leroy was too fast. He juked to the left and then to the right, and then faster than I thought possible, Leroy ducked down in a crouch and hammered my uncle time after time in the gut, like a punching bag. Uncle Freddy bowed over and spat on the sidewalk, and Tommy waded in. It wasn't a fair fight.

"Untie me," I said. Leroy left Tommy to my uncle and untied my hands. "He's got a gun," I said to Leroy.

We were just going to make sure it wouldn't be used when there was a loud bang and everything froze. I looked at Tommy, who was staring down in shock. The white T-shirt he was wearing blossomed red at the stomach. Uncle Freddy was on the ground, face bloody, pistol pointed at my brother. He looked shocked too. I ran to Tommy, who fell into my arms.

"Shit, Mikey, that hurts."

"It's okay, Tommy."

Apparently one of the neighbors had called the cops because there was a wail in the distance, and just like that, the cronies made a run for it, carrying off their broken comrades. When I looked up from my brother, Uncle Freddy was gone. Leroy went to the road to flag down the ambulance, and by the time the paramedics walked out to help, Tommy's eyes were fluttering closed.

"It's okay, Tommy," I kept saying. "It's going to be okay."

I don't know why I kept saying it, because I didn't feel it. Tommy reached out, grabbed the back of my head, and pulled me forward so that our foreheads touched. His lips moved, but he couldn't say anything, and then he fell limp, and my world crumbled inside.

Chapter 50

"I'm sorry, Doctor, can you say that again?" I asked.

The surgeon nodded patiently. "I won't lie to you, son. It doesn't look good. Your brother's lost a lot of blood. The bullet pierced multiple organs. We'll be in surgery for hours. I wanted to come out and let you know that we'll do the best we can."

"The best we can," I echoed.

The surgeon nodded, his face grave. "Make sure he has something to eat and drink if possible," the surgeon said to Leroy, meaning me.

"No problem, Doc. Thank you." Leroy put his arm around me. "It's going to be okay, man. I've got my whole family praying, and my mom's calling our preacher. They're going to get a prayer circle going for your brother."

I nodded, though I didn't really understand his words. Prayer circle wasn't really in my vocabulary. Wilbur Downs walked into the waiting room, arms stuffed with vending machine food.

"Here," he said, dumping it into Leroy's lap.

"Thanks, big brother," Leroy said. Downs grunted, snagged two candy bars, and went to join the rest of the team, who sat quietly a distance away. I looked over at them and nodded. If we hadn't bonded before, this would bond us forever.

The cops had shown up. In fact, it was the same cops who were there when I'd found Mrs. Mockingham. I was too much in shock to speak, so Leroy and Pip did all the talking.

There were threats from the cops, of course, something about us inciting a riot or some other nonsense, but in the end, Leroy said that it was late and that the cops didn't want to waste their time, especially since Uncle Freddy and his cronies had taken off.

Leroy handed me a Coke and some crackers, which I ate dutifully, though they tasted like nothing.

Mom was down the hall in the ICU. I should have gone to see her, but I didn't have the energy. I was guzzling the last bit of soda when Leroy nudged me. "Hey, I think this guy's here for you."

I looked up and, to my surprise, saw Mr. Romano standing hat in hand at the entrance of the waiting room.

Leroy rose. "Can I help you, sir?" he asked politely.

Mr. Romano said, "Would you gentlemen allow me to speak with Mr. Greco alone?"

Leroy looked to me, and I nodded. "Let's go, boys. Hey, Greco. We'll be right outside if you need us."

I saw that behind Mr. Romano were his men. They made no move to come inside. Downs patted me on the shoulder as he walked past, as did the rest of the team.

It was a strange sensation to have so many good men on my side. Leroy said Tommy was the one who'd called him in a panic, and just like that, Leroy rounded up the troops, and they headed to my hometown. How could I ever repay them for that? I didn't know. When they'd left the room, one of Mr. Romano's men closed the glazed door and put his back against it. It was just me and Johnny Cheese. He sat down next to me. He looked more withered than the last time that I'd seen him.

"I'm sorry about your mother and your brother," he said.

"Thank you," I said.

"This business with your uncle"—he shook his head—"it's bad business. Tell me why it happened."

I couldn't tell him the whole truth, so I told him part of it, the part that I knew he would understand. "The ledger, Mr. Romano. Freddy took the ledger."

The old man nodded. "Then it's a good thing I came tonight. You wouldn't want to come empty handed tomorrow, now would you?"

I shook my head. "No, sir."

"And your friends, the football players, did you call them?"

I shook my head. "Tommy did, sir. They came to help."

"They don't owe you anything?"

I shook my head again. "No, sir. They're my friends."

He nodded knowingly. "It's good to have loyal friends, men who will stand with you no matter the cost. Did you know that I served in the Second Great War?"

"No, sir."

He nodded, taking a moment to look up at the ceiling to gather his thoughts. "I was young and foolish. It was in the army that I learned true loyalty. It was also in the army that I learned the breadth of man's evil. It hardened my heart in many ways, but it also taught me that if you want something, you have to fight for it."

He chuckled. "I was there when we liberated the death camps. You've never seen such misery. And yet those men and women clung to life like I cling to it now. It bred in me a toughness that I will bring when I meet heaven or hell. I don't know which. I say all this so that you understand that I'm an honest man in my own way. Maybe not in the ways of polite society, but I have rarely wronged an innocent, and I promise you that until I take my last breath, I will tell you the truth. Now, Mr. Greco, I expect the same courtesy. So why don't you tell me why it is that your uncle attacked his own kin? Because in my world, such a thing is a mortal sin, and as long as I have breath left in my soul, I will not let such a sin go unpunished."

Chapter 51

I didn't know what else to tell him. There was no way in hell I was going to give him the information imparted by good ol' Uncle Freddy. That would probably see me taken out back and shot.

When it was obvious that I didn't have a reply, Mr. Romano continued. "Would you indulge an old man and let me tell you another story about the Great War?" I nodded.

He sat back in the chair and closed his eyes. When he opened them again, and this may sound strange, but he looked like a younger man, at least in his eyes, like he was looking back in time. And back in time was where he took me.

"They taught me many things in the army. How to shoot guns, how to jump out of planes, how to use a radio, how to drive a Jeep. I picked up languages along the way. I guess you could say I had a knack for it. I became useful. Inside me grew a new respect and pride for my country."

Mr. Romano nodded, smiling at the memory.

"I loved my time in the army. I was trusted, depended upon. For me, the end of the war came too soon. I got my orders home. I tried to reenlist, but the drawdown came quickly. My time in the service to my country came to an end. My seeming savior appeared in the form of a man I'd met in Naples, Italy. He was with army intelligence, and he used me on a handful of occasions as an interpreter. I wouldn't say that we were friends, but he knew I was a hard worker. When we ran into each other at the commissary, he was surprised that I was still in the army.

"I asked him what his plans were, and he told me that he was going into law enforcement. He was one of those fellows who always seemed to have the right plan. I didn't see him for another five years, five years where I struggled to reintegrate with normal American life. I bagged groceries, I pumped gas, I worked construction. I mowed lawns with one of those push mowers that now you only punish children with when they've been bad. No gas, no engine, only your muscles. And eventually, I did have to go home. There were too many returning veterans to compete with. After many nudges in that direction, I knew that the only place that would welcome me was my hometown.

"I came home to find that my father died of a heart attack not long after I'd left for the war. My mother was taking in tenants at our house. When she saw me, she did not embrace her long-lost son. Instead, she put me to work, ordering me around like I was thirteen again. What else was I to do? I made the beds and chopped onions for the meals. I took out the trash and made sure that our tenants behaved. When I could sneak away, I went to the library. I would hide there and read books for free. I'd become a voracious reader in the army. It was my only lifeline. One day as I was walking home with an armful of books, my old friend appeared, as if God himself had snapped his fingers, and poof, there he was. I still remember that he wore a brown suit—a strange detail to remember, I know. But for some reason, that brown suit meant something to me. That, and his hat. He looked official.

"He took me to lunch and asked me all about what I'd been up to since leaving the army. I told him, and then I asked if he'd heard anything about the army taking veterans back in their ranks. I told him I would go back in as a private, that I didn't care, that I needed to get away. He shook his head sadly. 'I'm sorry, Johnny.' That's what he called me, Johnny. 'But I might have something else for you.' He didn't tell me what that was, but he promised to keep in touch. His visits became a regular thing. I looked forward to them. They were my respite from a sad life. Gradually, he told me that he was working from Chicago, but that he'd make frequent trips to New York City. He didn't tell me who he worked for until one night when he met me at a small restaurant outside town. It's not there now, but it was a place with dark corners where friends could get reacquainted. He told me he worked for the FBI, and I immediately asked him how I could join. He shook his head at the idea, told me that I wasn't qualified. I still remember that feeling of rejection. 'But I might have something else for you,' he said. 'It won't be easy, and you probably won't like it.' I pressed him, made him tell me, and eventually he did, though reluctantly. He hesitated because he knew my spirit, he knew my honesty, my straightforward approach to life. And in those next words, my whole life changed."

Chapter 52

Mr. Romano told me how his old friend recruited him to be an informant, that organized crime was on the rise, and that he, Mr. Romano's friend, was on the front lines of that fight.

"He told me that if I could keep my eyes and ears open that there might be opportunity. I was naive. He explained the basic criminal organization, at least of what they understood, and made certain suggestions on how I should get in bed with the fellows in town, make the connections, all the way to Chicago. That would take time.

"I soon made a reputation for getting things done. Small deliveries here, messages passed there, but I was reliable, had served honorably in the army. I was a man to be trusted. There were things I had to do along the way that once disgusted me. I have become used to such things. I've been shot three times. I have killed men with my own hands, all with the blessing of our great Uncle Sam."

He shook his head and wiped a hand across his forehead. I hadn't noticed that he was sweating despite how cold it was in the waiting room.

"Mr. Romano, can I get you some water or . . ."

He shook his head. "No, I'm fine, but thank you. Let me continue while I have the energy." He coughed into a handkerchief and went on. "With my friend's help, I was able to rise through the ranks, as they say, with continued successes and the intelligence I was able to provide. My friend rose as well. He kept me close. I was his source, and he never divulged my name to another soul in the FBI. We were careful, more so as the years went by. He was offered a promotion. They wanted him in Miami, where the import of illicit substances was becoming a problem. My friend and I had a plan. He was the only man in the world who knew the truth of my life. When I was with him, I could relax, be myself and not the character that I had built through toil and pain.

"We had a goal. We would take down organized crime piece by piece. Once that was done, we would leave, find a quiet town out west, and settle down to our books and good whiskey.

"Neither of us married. We figured that was for the best. And then one day I opened the paper. I have read it every morning since it happened. On the third page, there was a picture of my friend, his official FBI picture. The article said my friend had been killed in a raid. At first, I could not believe it. I read the article many times, wishing, hoping that it was someone else.

"For months, I waited, assuming that I would get a call from my friend's successor, but I never did. No one knew of my existence but him. And he was gone. That was a dark time for me. Those were the years that I earned my reputation for ruthlessness. Something changed in me, something that I hope you never experience, because it broke my soul."

Mr. Romano sat back in his chair again and closed his eyes. When he reopened them, he was an older man again. "I tell you all this for one reason and one reason alone—other than my friend and yourself, there is only one man in the world who ever heard my story."

I figured he was going to say another army buddy or maybe a shrink. His next words shocked me to my core.

"Michael, it was your father who I told. It was your father who became a friend. It was your father who died because of me."

Chapter 53

I sat there in shock, not knowing what to say. "When I first met your father, he was not much older than you. He was full of spirit, but he was hardheaded. I could see that he was running down the wrong path. Sprinting was more like it." He shook his head at the memory.

"He'd gotten a reputation for stealing cars. The fancier, the better. He would have a buddy drop him off in downtown Chicago, and he would reappear here two hours later with a shiny new Cadillac. I knew it was only a matter of time before the police, or worse, the FBI, got to him. So, I had a conversation with your father. I kept my eye on him.

"His brother, your uncle Freddy, was already running with the wrong crowd, and I told him to stay clear, that that young boy was nothing but trouble. I saw it in his eyes. Freddy's vices are power and greed. But man cannot dissuade heavenly fate or the devil. Your father was pulled into this world, much to my disappointment. Rather than fight it—that would be a fool's goal—I pulled him closer. He met your mother, and you were born. He was so proud. I wish you could have seen the way he doted on you. When you were baptized, I stood at the back of the church, smiling at your father's happiness. You were six months old when he came to me and told me that he wanted to leave. I asked him where he wanted to go, and he said Alaska.

"I told him to be serious, and he said he was. He left for a year and came back with fists full of cash. Your father was many things, but he was not good with his money. The money was gone in months. Once again, he came to me and told me that he was going to leave. I said no. I demanded that he not leave you and your mother. I remember him telling me that there was nothing I could do to stop him. I grasped at the only thread I could. I told him my story, told him my plans for reconnecting with the FBI, and that he, your father, could be the man to change everything, and that we would work together. That by the time you were in high school, you all would move to a new town, live a new life, that everything would be different. To your father's credit, he took to the new task with relish.

"We had to be careful. I instructed him each step of the way, showed him how to work slowly, showed him exactly what kind of information the FBI would want, what could link something back to him and what would not. Your father was a brilliant student. But the pressures of marriage and fatherhood were too much. He started cutting corners. He would take side jobs to make extra money. He had no patience. He led two lives, sometimes three. He was his own man, and by the time I had a plan to get him out—to get you all out—he was dead. Gone. Our plans destroyed. And here we sit now, Michael, two men covered in pain and years of regret. I will be gone soon. You have many years ahead of you. God willing, you have a choice to make, my friend.

"I can help you disappear. I can give you the money to do that. You can leave and never look back, or you can stay and fight. It's your decision. You don't strike me as a man who will go to the authorities, and I will tell you that if you do, it will be the wrong decision. This is a decision to be made between men, men of faith, and men of honor."

He paused to let his incredible tale sink in.

"What do you say, Michael? Can I help you build a new life? Because I would like nothing but to see you happy. Pick a city, and I will send you there with enough means to survive. Or you stay."

I didn't have to think about it.

Something had been building inside me as he was telling his tale. Something had been building inside me for a long time. It was like a story that needed a final ending. The perfect punch line, no cliff-hangers. I looked at Mr. Romano, and I said, "Tell me what I need to do, Mr. Romano. Tell me how I can ensure my family's safety."

Chapter 54

Uncle Freddy's caravan of cronies pulled up to the abandoned gas station like it was escorting a dead body to a funeral, slowly and cautiously. I leaned against the old pump, taking another pull from the cigarette, my hands surprisingly steady. Freddy wasn't taking any chances. Four goons got out of a car; two patted me down. The other two went looking around the old gas station. When they reemerged, one nodded to the third vehicle in the five-vehicle convoy, and Uncle Freddy emerged. He had a bandage on the side of his neck and a black eye. He walked with a little bit of a limp, but even a limp couldn't wipe away his bravado.

"You shouldn't be smoking those things, kid. They'll kill you."

In response, I flicked the almost finished cigarette away and pulled out another. He slapped it out of my hand, and I let him.

"I said those things will kill you, kid."

"You said that before."

We stared at each other for a long time. His face softened. "I'm sorry about your brother. It shouldn't have gone down that way."

I didn't reply. I figured no reply was needed.

"Is he going to live?" Uncle Freddy asked.

I shrugged.

"Is that all you got, Greco? A shrug for your baby brother."

"What do you want me to say, Uncle Freddy? That I'm all torn up inside? That you ripped out my heart and stomped it into smithereens? Is that what you want me to say?"

Uncle Freddy shook his head. "You've got some balls, kid. I'll give you that." He turned to one of his thugs. "He clean?"

"He's clean," the crony said, picking up the cigarette that had been slapped out of my hand and lighting it for himself.

"Why'd you ask me here, Greco?" Uncle Freddy asked.

"You were surprised when I called," I said.

Freddy nodded.

"I'm done fighting. I'm tired," I said. "I'll give you anything you want."

Uncle Freddy's eyes lit up at that, like all his plans were finally coming to fruition. He snapped his fingers and beckoned for one of his cronies. "Take the others and do a wide sweep of the area. I want to make sure we're not being watched."

The men hurried to their task, leaving us two Grecos alone.

"I have a present for you," I said.

"If it's another cigarette, I don't want it," Uncle Freddy said.

"No. It's something better. Something you'll like."

"Tell me kid, because we ain't getting any younger."

Mr. Romano had guided me. He'd said that I needed to do what I needed to do, so I did that now. I leaned forward, and Uncle Freddy backed away.

"What? You think I'm going to bite you?" I asked.

"It's happened before," Uncle Freddy said.

I laughed. "I promise not to bite you. Pinkie swear." I held up my pinky.

Freddy grunted and leaned forward. Then I whispered in his ear and told him the truth, or at least the specific truth that I thought he wanted to hear. When we parted, he whistled.

"Will that get me and my family off the hook?" I asked.

Uncle Freddy crossed his arms across his widening chest. "Yeah, kid, that'll get you off the hook."

My legs wanted to go wobbly from relief. Mr. Romano had suggested offering himself up for sacrifice. He wouldn't be long in this

189

world anyway. His words, not mine. He told me that he was dying, that all the treatments hadn't worked. In fact, they'd probably cut his time on earth by at least half.

"I owe this to you and to your father, Michael," he told me.

I don't know what I expected, but I made another suggestion. Uncle Freddy had asked for Dad's Bible before. The only way to fully decrypt the stolen ledger.

"I'll go back to school," I said. "I'll bring back the codebook next weekend."

I thought it was a fair deal. Let Freddy deal with the aftermath. Get my family out of it.

Uncle Freddy grunted again. "You know what, kid? I appreciate you helping me out like this."

He leaned forward, and quicker than his bulk suggested, slammed a fist into my gut. I doubled over involuntarily. While I was regaining my breath, he whispered in my ear, "We don't need your daddy's book anymore." He pressed in closer, and I felt his lips on my ear. "I'm the one with the FBI on a string now, and you're not going anywhere until we put Mr. Romano in the ground."

Chapter 55

As the caravan drove lazily into town, past the drugstore, past the bank, past my old high school, I wondered if my family was cursed. It sure as hell seemed that way. If Dad really had tried to do the right thing and been killed for it, what did that leave me? I am not a superstitious man by nature, but sometimes a whole lot of coincidences lump up to be one big fat reality.

"Drop us off up here," Uncle Freddy said to the driver. The car pulled up to the curb, and Uncle Freddy pulled me outside. "Come on," he said, walking quickly. It took me a second to realize where we were. It was an old neighborhood where most of the houses sat deserted. The kids in town said the place was haunted by ghosts.

We walked through a front yard, the waist-high grass the only thing impeding our way. Walked through the side yard, a backyard, and into the back of an abandoned house.

"You keep your mouth shut unless I tell you to talk. You got that?" Uncle Freddy told me.

"Sure," I said.

We walked over discarded debris. A cat bolted out the window. Uncle Freddy knocked twice on a door. I heard a muffled "Come." He opened the door, and we walked down a set of stairs into the basement.

There was a nondescript man sitting on a tattered chair. He looked up as we entered the room. "Who's this?" the man asked.

"A witness," Uncle Freddy said. The man made a face like this wasn't the plan. I didn't say anything. "I need your blessing," Uncle Freddy said.

"My blessing for what?"

"We're going to do some things. I need to make sure that you guys are going to look the other way."

"What kind of things?" the man asked.

Uncle Freddy shrugged. "Little things. Things you don't need to worry about."

"Does he know who I am?" the man asked, pointing at me.

"Nephew, meet the FBI. FBI, this is my nephew."

I didn't say anything because that's what Uncle Freddy had ordered. But I couldn't believe that the FBI would choose him to be an informant. Talk about a bad investment.

"I need your word that you're not going to step in. Not until I tell you to," Uncle Freddy said.

"You know that's not the way this works," the man said.

Uncle Freddy laughed. "You think you know how this works, but I'm going to tell you something. I'm about to make you a famous man in the bureau. I'm about to crack this town—hell, Chicago—wide open. What do you say to that?"

"I'd say that's a big promise," the man said. "Why should I believe you?"

"Because I've got the goods," Uncle Freddy said.

"Are you saying this kid is the goods?"

"He's part of it."

The man exhaled. "Fine. You do what you need to do. I'll cover for you."

Uncle Freddy slapped his hands together. Both me and Mr. FBI flinched. "Hot damn," Uncle Freddy said.

"Will there be anything else?" Mr. FBI asked.

"No, that's it." Uncle Freddy grabbed my arm and turned us both toward the stairs. But then he turned back to Mr. FBI and said, "There is something else. The next time you see me, I want you to call me Mr. Greco."

Chapter 56

Uncle Freddy looked like a kid who'd been picked to swim with Shamu. He was so giddy when we got back to the car, he asked the driver for a chill pill. I didn't know what that was, but a pill was produced, and Uncle Freddy chewed it up and swallowed it dry.

On the way back to the car, Uncle Freddy had warned me again not to say anything about the FBI because if I did, he'd shoot me in the head. "Besides, the FBI's seen you now. They know who you are. So that's my insurance policy. One of many." He chuckled at that, like he knew anything about insurance.

We left the deserted neighborhood and headed farther outside town. I had an idea where we were going, though I didn't know the exact way. I'd been blindfolded the last time. We were on a rural road now. The convoy took a left and then a right. It had beams illuminating nothing but blacktop and fields for miles. It was hours until sunrise. I was cold, so cold. I clamped my hands to my thighs to keep myself from shivering. I didn't want to show any weakness.

We pulled up to a modest home. Its Victorian architecture, elegant during its time, was dated for 1989. The lawn was as perfect as the white picket fence.

Men piled out of the other cars first, and Uncle Freddy and I stayed put with our driver. It took five minutes. A crony appeared and gave Uncle Freddy a thumbs-up.

"Let's go kid," Uncle Freddy said, pulling me unnecessarily from the car. We walked up the steps, Uncle Freddy marching like a conquering hero. We walked through the living room, which I now recognized. Down a hall and into a bedroom where there was a hospital bed in the middle and IV bags and hospital machinery lined neatly along the wall. And there, sitting in a leather recliner, was Mr. Romano. He did not look at me. He looked straight at Uncle Freddy.

"What is this?" Mr. Romano asked, his face not giving away an ounce of anxiety. "Where are my men?"

"They took the night off," Uncle Freddy said. If Mr. Romano was afraid, he didn't show it.

"And why is the boy here?" Mr. Romano asked.

"He's a witness."

"A witness to what?"

Uncle Freddy pulled the pistol from his waistband. "You ever read about regime change, Mr. Romano?" Mr. Romano did not answer. "I'll take that as a no, so let me explain it to you. You see, every once in a while, a president, an emperor, a dictator, they've had their time in the sun, you see? And the powers that be"—he pointed to himself—"that would be me today. We see it as our duty to change the leadership. They freshen up the place, if you take my meaning."

"You are here to kill me?" Mr. Romano said.

"Yeah, sure, we'll get to that. But first I want you to admit something."

"And what is that?"

"I want you to admit that I won."

"Why would I do that?"

Uncle Freddy laughed. "Because I'm sitting here pointing a gun at you, not the other way around."

"I've had many guns pointed to me," Mr. Romano said. "You think you're original, Manfredo, but you're not."

"Oh, and who was? My brother?"

"Your brother was a better man than you. Your brother was a man of integrity, a man of honor."

Uncle Freddy hooted at that. "That's a good one, Mr. Romano. A really good one. A real knee-slapper. So, you're saying a man of honor, a man of integrity, leaves his wife and kids, makes them sleep on family's couches, doesn't give them enough money for food? You're saying that's a man of honor, of integrity?"

"I did not say that he was a perfect man."

"You got that right, at least," Uncle Freddy said. "Go ahead, kid." He nudged me. "Tell him all about your dad. Tell him about your Mayberry upbringing, how the four of you used to walk hand in hand down Main Street eating ice cream, telling stories about how swell life was."

I didn't say anything. Uncle Freddy put the gun to my head. "Go ahead, kid. Tell us all those swell stories."

"Leave the boy out of this," Mr. Romano said. The pistol swiveled back to the dying man.

I'm not going to explain this accurately because I'm not sure words can. He sat there in his nightshirt, bone thin and old. But I could feel the power, the absolute certainty coming from Mr. Romano. And that power and dignity helped me stand firm.

"You turned my brother against me," Uncle Freddy said. "We used to be two peas in a pod, inseparable."

"It sounds like you are rewriting history," Mr. Romano said.

"What the fuck do you know about history?"

"I've lived it, Manfredo. We must learn from it."

"Oh yeah? And what the hell is history going to say when they find out that you were a snitch? That you turned my brother too? That everything you built here is a lie?"

Mr. Romano didn't flinch. "Are you saying you are a better man, Manfredo? Is that what you're telling me? Is that the lecture you've come to my house at this hour of the night to provide?"

Uncle Freddy didn't laugh. He took a step closer to Mr. Romano. I expected more diatribe. I expected Uncle Freddy to prop himself up with bravado at level ten. But instead he said, "No, Mr. Romano. I came to give you this."

And before anyone could react, the pistol came up and fired two times straight into Mr. Romano's forehead.

Chapter 57

"That's what you get, you old bastard," Uncle Freddy said, and then he emptied his magazine into Mr. Romano's chest. When his chamber clicked empty, he spat on the old man for good measure. "Go to hell."

As if in response, the body shifted and slid off one side of the chair, thumping to the floor with the finality of death.

"What the . . . ?" Uncle Freddy walked forward and bent down. I had to step to the side to see what he was doing. A phone receiver had been wedged behind Mr. Romano. As we both stared down at it, the earpiece started beeping to tell us that the call, whoever it had been with, was disconnected.

Chapter 58

Uncle Freddy ripped the phone from the wall and threw it across the room. No sooner had its remnants hit the ground than we both heard it—sirens coming closer. He went to the window, and I could see the lights, flashing blue and red, over his shoulder.

"What the fuck? What the fuck?" Uncle Freddy murmured. He whirled on me. "You. You did this."

I put my hands in the air. "It wasn't me, I swear. I didn't know about it."

He looked to the dead man on the ground. Like an idiot, he pulled the trigger, forgetting that it was empty. He fumbled with a new magazine, tossing the spent one away. Then he thought better of it and picked it up and shoved it in his pocket. He made sure he couldn't be seen through the curtain and peered out again. More ominous sounds—helicopters, a voice over a megaphone. Uncle Freddy backed away from the window in shock.

That's when I ran. I didn't know where I was going. I couldn't go outside and risk being killed. The sound of the descending helicopter was like the roar of heaven. It masked my stomping feet. I found a broom closet, put myself in, hid behind whatever I could find, and wrapped my arms around my legs. I thought I heard Uncle Freddy following me, foot stomps all around.

I don't know how long it was. More foot stomps, and then I heard someone say, "All clear."

Shit. All clear, except for me. What was I supposed to do? My heart hammered. The next part I had to take slowly. Last thing I wanted was to come out of the closet and get shot.

"I'm in here," I called out. "I'm in here."

It didn't take them long. Soon there was a weapon pointed at me and a blaring flashlight that I couldn't see through.

"You armed, kid?" the man said.

"No, sir."

"Let me see your hands."

I put my hands in the air.

"All right. Come out, slowly."

I did as instructed, moving inch by inch.

"It's okay. You can put your arms down."

I did, with relief. There were men in black milling about. Someone else walked up.

"You Michael Greco?"

"Yes, sir," I said in surprise.

"Come on. Boss wants to see you." He led me out of the house, but not before walking by Mr. Romano's room. Someone was taking pictures. The flashes from the camera reminded me of a scene from old Hollywood, Mr. Romano's last act.

The boss was a middle-aged guy who was sitting on the swing on the front porch. "This the kid you looking for, boss?"

The man looked up. He had sharp piercing eyes that I figured were perfect for interrogation. "You the one they call Greco?" the man asked.

"Yes, sir."

"Have a seat."

I sat down next to him on the swing, and for a time we just sat there. Then he asked, "You okay?"

"Yes, sir. I think so."

"Because we can get you to a therapist if you want."

"No, sir. I think I'm fine, at least for now."

"Take it from my experience, kid. You start having crazy dreams, you go talk to somebody. Lost a lot of buddies after Vietnam because they were too proud to get help. Not me. I knew I was about to swallow a bullet or else I wouldn't have gotten help."

"Yes, sir," I said, not really knowing what else to say. This was the weirdest Folgers moment I'd ever had. A question came to me, the answer I had to know. "Did you kill my uncle?"

The man was watching his team load Freddy's pals into the back of a van. "Not yet, but I don't think he'll get far. That agent he introduced you to. He's one of mine. We've had our eyes on Manfredo Greco for months. Thought he was playing his own game. Didn't know we were already working with Mr. Romano, God rest his soul." He snapped his fingers. "Oh hell, I almost forgot." He reached inside his FBI windbreaker and pulled out an envelope. "This is for you, kid."

"Who's it from?" I asked.

The man gestured to the house. I took his point. It was from Mr. Romano. I tore open the envelope and pulled out the single sheet of paper. The letter read:

> Michael,
> I'm sorry I couldn't help you sooner. I'm sorry I couldn't help your father, but please take this as my final gift to you. Your freedom, your family's freedom. Get away from this place. Find a pretty young girl, get married, have children. Do all the things that your father and I never did.
>
> Always remember to be a good man, to be an honest man, to work hard, and to remember the gifts we've been given by this country. I wish you good luck young man.

It was signed "Giancarlo."

"Have you read this?" I asked.

The man shrugged, as if it were obvious. He was the FBI. "When you're done with it, we need to burn it."

"Burn it?" I asked.

"Can't have any evidence, kid. You really want to be linked back to this mess?"

"No, sir."

"Good."

"Can I read it one more time?"

The man nodded and waited for me. Then I handed him the envelope and the letter. He pulled out a lighter and, right there on the porch, burned them both.

"What happens next?" I asked.

"Three things actually. One, your brother's gonna make a full recovery."

My body was flooded with relief. I didn't know what to say.

"Two, your mother's been asking for you. Says she's ready to get clean. We're happy to help with that."

"And the third thing?" I asked, too full of gratitude to say much more.

"Our mutual friend wants you to get back to school. Says you've been a little distracted, said you might need a ride."

"Could I see my mother and brother first?"

He rose from the swing. "Of course, we're the FBI, kid, not the IRS. We still have a heart."

Chapter 59

The FBI agent never gave me his name. He did give me one of those classic movie lines, something like "If we need you, we'll find you." Mom was sitting up in bed when they took me to the hospital. She hugged me and kept saying she was sorry. I kept telling her it was okay, that it wasn't her fault. But she said it was and that she was ready to get help. She entered rehab the next day.

As for Tommy, the tough bastard was already joking with Leroy and the rest of the team when I arrived.

"You got to check this out," he said, lifting up the sheet and showing off the array of bandages across his torso.

Until Uncle Freddy was caught, the FBI and the local police would keep an eye on my family. The agent had made a tentative plan. Then once my mother was finished with rehab, making meetings, and Tommy was healed, they'd move into a little house purchased by Mr. Romano, another gift for my family and me. They'd be ten minutes from school. And though that's not how I would've wanted it before, that's how I wanted it now.

It was Sunday night when the trucks that had brought my teammates pulled out of my hometown and headed back to school. Leroy and Pip chatted incessantly, and I listened. It turned out that I'd given everyone the adventure of their lifetimes. I wanted to be a normal kid again. Hell, I would've been happy to be relegated to water boy if it meant living a normal life.

I didn't wait until morning to see Coach. I called his house, and he agreed to meet me at his office. There, I told him everything about my father, the rest of my family, Uncle Freddy, and the FBI. Why? Because he'd earned my trust, and I knew he wouldn't tell a soul. And he never did. He clapped me on the back as he walked me out the door.

"I'm proud of you, son," he said.

"Thanks, Coach."

My next stop was obvious. I had to see Sheila. At first, I didn't think she was home. She didn't answer when I rang the doorbell. But then after the third ring, lights went on in the house, and I saw her walking down the stairs in her pajamas. She opened the door, and there are no words to describe that smile. She looked tired, and her color was off. But to me, she was beautiful. We spent that night lying on the couch, talking, catching up. I told her everything too. When the sun finally peaked over the horizon, she was asleep on my lap, and I was the happiest man in the world.

Sheila's eyes fluttered open.

"Is it morning already?" she asked.

"It is," I said. "Mind if I make some coffee?"

"Only if you make me some," she said. "I'm going to go get dressed. You remember where everything is?"

I nodded. She rose and kissed me on the lips.

"I'm glad you're here," she said.

"I'm glad I'm here," I said. "Now, go get dressed. I need caffeine."

She headed to the bedroom, and I headed to the kitchen. The adrenaline of the past two days had run their course. Truth be told, I was bone tired. I would need two pots of coffee to keep me going today. It took me a minute to remember where the filters were. But as I finally got the coffee brewing, I scrounged the fridge for leftovers, realizing I was ravenous. I was putting my dish in the sink when I heard footsteps. I turned, ready to hold Sheila again, only it wasn't Sheila. It was a battered and disheveled Uncle Freddy. My heart rose into my throat.

"What are you doing here?" I asked.

C. G. Cooper

"I'm here for my pound of flesh," he said.

My eyes flickered to the hallway, and Uncle Freddy grinned.

"Don't worry. She's fine, for now."

"Don't touch her," I said.

"That's up to you, nephew."

"What do you want?"

"I told you. I want my pound of flesh."

The now-familiar pistol came out of his pocket. I took him in, his stained shirt, his scuffed shoes, his messed up hair. There were cuts all up and down his forearms and around the side of his face, not to mention the black eye.

A plan formed in my mind. I wasn't afraid. Not for me. I stood straight and took a step forward.

My plan was simple: rush my uncle. Maybe I'd get shot in the process, but I'd wrestle that pistol from his grip and shoot him too. I was sorry for how that might leave things with Sheila, but I was young. And if Tommy had been shot, maybe I could get shot too. Sure, I was taking a chance, a big chance. But what the hell else was I going to do?

The pistol shook in Uncle Freddy's hand, but it still came up.

"You've been a pain in my ass since before I can remember," he said.

"At least that's one thing we've got in common," I replied.

He sneered, but it didn't have the effect on me that it used to. His eyes were bloodshot. Every time he spoke, spittle came out. He was the shell of a desperate man.

"You think you're some hotshot," he said. "God's gift to the Greco clan."

His finger tightened on the trigger. I had to time this just right. I thought about Leroy and how he would juke left and right. The skills would surely take him to the NFL. Better give a prayer of thanks for my friend. I willed that I would have his strength for what was to come.

He was about to say something else, something no doubt filled with venom and stemming from a life of regret, when I rushed him.

204

But I never made it to Uncle Freddy. A loud boom threatened to shatter my eardrums. And instead of feeling pain, I watched Uncle Freddy sink to the floor and a familiar ledger fall from a pocket. His hand with the pistol came up from the ground, shaking wildly. Another boom, and the hand fell. Uncle Freddy moved no more.

My eyes drifted from Uncle Freddy's body up to a now-dressed Sheila holding a shotgun. And a single curl of smoke looped from the barrel up to the ceiling.

Epilogue

I'd like to tell you that everything was hunky-dory after that, but the facts still remained. Uncle Freddy was gone. My family was safe, thanks to the ledger Uncle Freddy brought to our final confrontation. I gave it to the FBI, and they used it to build cases against many of Dad's former associates. It was Tommy who came up with the idea that kept us safe. "Pin it all on Uncle Freddy," he'd said in front the FBI team assigned to our case. And that's what they did. They donated his body to a medical school and carefully let word slip that Uncle Freddy was now in federal witness protection. That seemed to convince Dad's former associates that Uncle Freddy was the man behind the investigations and raid, not the star college football player and his family.

The Jefferson State football team lost in a nail-biter after all was said and done. We did not make it to the bowl game, but what we did get was a promotion to Division I. The next year we would play against the likes of Ohio State and Michigan.

I got three more wonderful months with Sheila, where we shared many moments and memories. We stayed up late, talking for hours. She told me that she'd majored in psychology because she wanted to be a counselor for cancer survivors. She said that she'd fallen for me because I had sad, hopeful eyes. She dreamed of the day when her body wouldn't hurt anymore. Mostly I just listened. When I wasn't going to class or attending spring practice, I was with her. She slept in my arms, and I breathed in her soul.

Sometimes we'd invite Leroy and the rest of the gang to hang out at Sheila's house. She threw lavish parties, black-tie events, costume parties, everything she'd never done. And when the night was over, she would fall asleep in my arms, too tired to speak.

She died on a Tuesday. Her mother was there, and her father had just gone out for groceries. I was in class. Mrs. Sinclair called me, and it was the first time I heard her without poise. They let me see her body before the hearse took it away. I said my goodbye then. Her funeral was a small service, exactly what Sheila had requested. I took four people with me—Leroy, Pip, Tommy, and Coach Grant. Tommy had met Sheila, of course, but my mom was still in and out of rehab. It would take three stints for sobriety to finally stick, at least shakily. After the funeral, the Sinclairs put their house on the market, but they kept in touch. They always send a Christmas card and call me on my birthday. They didn't owe me that, but maybe they thought that talking to me was like talking to some last part of their daughter. They're still around and living in a retirement community in Jupiter, Florida.

As for the football team, we went on to win conference championships the next three years. Leroy would get his starting spot as running back. Wilbur Downs got drafted by the Green Bay Packers and would go on to protect Brett Favre, the future Football Hall of Famer. Pip graduated at the top of our class, of course, and spent the next ten years hopping from football team to football team, known as one of the longest kickers in NFL history. He could have played longer, but he took what money he'd made and began building a massive real estate empire.

Leroy and I were inseparable. I, the quarterback. He, my running back. We roomed together for four years. When his mother died, I was there for him, like he'd been there for me. He dedicated his last season at Jefferson State to her memory and went on to shatter many records. Tragically, Leroy was killed a week before graduation. He'd just gotten into Officer Candidates School and was going to become an officer in the Marine Corps. He'd stopped at a local convenience store on his way back to campus. It was late, and when a guy high on meth came in the convenience store, waving a gun around, Leroy immediately went into protection mode, shielding a pregnant mother. Leroy was shot three times protecting her. She and her baby came out unscathed. They never found the gunman, who got away with a fist full of cash and a bag of Doritos.

It felt like the entire student body was at his funeral. No one cried more than I did. Well, maybe Wilbur Downs, who sat in the front row, refusing to leave when the service was over. His arm cradled the casket, and his large tears soaked the shining wood. It was Coach Grant who finally pried the big man from his little brother. Graduation was a somber affair without Leroy, but I refused to be down. Leroy wouldn't have wanted it that way, and neither would've Sheila.

Tommy started at Jefferson State the next year. He'd gone on to do well in high school, though he had a lot of catching up to do, and Coach Grant told me that an anonymous donor had paid for his tuition. I have no idea who that anonymous donor was. At first, I thought it was Coach or maybe the Sinclairs. But when I asked them each, slyly, of course no one admitted to it. And then on the day that I was packing up my belongings to finally move out into the real world, a courier arrived.

"Michael Greco," the man asked.

"That's me," I said.

"Sign here, please." I signed his pad of paper, and he handed me a small envelope. "Have a good day," the courier said. "Greco" was written on the outside of the envelope. I opened it quickly and found a sheet of paper with familiar handwriting. My heart leaped.

> Greco,
> If you're reading this, then our mutual friend deemed it necessary, and it probably means that I'm dead. I wanted you to have this letter so that you know how sorry I am for not being there for you. You needed a good dad and what I gave you fell short. All I can

say is that I thought I was doing the right thing. I wanted to be the hero. Maybe it was my ego, or maybe I was trying to protect you and your mother and your brother. I don't think there ever was a concrete reason. I'm not a perfect man. I never have been. Too many bad habits.

I hope that you can be better than me. I challenge you to see the good in people, to find the light in the world instead of the darkness. (I learned that from Mr. Romano) Do not lie, cheat or steal. Work hard. Prove yourself. Show the world that you are a man to be trusted and admired. Never forget your friends and know that your family is only your family for as long as they prove to be so.

There are so many mistakes I made with your mom, but I wouldn't change it because you and your brother wouldn't be here. I take the blame. Your mom and I just didn't fit. That wasn't her fault. I made a lot of promises that didn't pan out. I won't ask you to tell her I'm sorry. That's my job, one I hope to get to before I die.

I'm sure if you're reading this, you've grown to be the man that I never was, the man that I tried to be. Know that I'm looking down on you right now and that if you ever need to talk to me, all you have to do is ask, because I'll be right there with you forever, son. And I hope that one day you can forgive me and that one day, a long, long time in the future, when you've lived a wonderful life, that we can meet up in heaven and maybe toss the football. What do you say, son? You throw, and I'll go long.

Love, Dad

I pull that letter out every time life seems too tough. Every time I got knocked down. When I started my own company, I would stay up late, sick with worry that I wouldn't be able to make payroll, that I wouldn't be able to pay the mortgage on the house. In each instance, my father was there with me.

As for me, I've done okay. I got married. I've got three amazing boys. They're all out of the house now, and I'm not embarrassed to say that I cried like a baby when they each left. I look back at 1989, and now that there's been some time, I see that it wasn't all pain. There were lessons there, things that I pulled when times got harder, when my mom relapsed again, or when I had to call Pip and ask him if he wanted to be one of my investors. I was afraid every time, but at least I knew that I wasn't alone because that's what those years taught me, that to be alone is to die. And that if you don't ask for help, especially from the ones who love you the most, then why the hell are we really here?

So how about I leave you with that? The fact that as I move forward into the next phase of my life, I plan to be a better friend, a better husband, and a world-class father. I think I've been all those things, but I can always be better. I do it for my dad. I do it for Mr. Romano. I do it for Leroy and everyone else who saw something in me that I couldn't see in myself. Because if life isn't about having faith in yourself, then what is it really? I, for one, refuse to live in fear. I choose to hold my head high, to pull up those around me, to see the best in the world, and to always, always remember what I've been given.

Acknowledgments

Thanks to Honoree Corder for hosting the dinner where I met Danielle Marshall. Danielle, thank you for seeing the magic in this story and understanding (maybe better than I did) the road less traveled, on which I was about to embark. I won't forget it.

About the Author

C. G. Cooper is the *USA Today* and Amazon bestselling author of more than twenty-five thrillers, including the Corps Justice series, several spin-offs, and stand-alone novels.

Drawing on his time as an infantry officer in the United States Marine Corps—after earning a degree in foreign affairs from the University of Virginia—Cooper sifted his experience through his vivid imagination in *Corps Justice*, the first novel in the beloved series. Book nine of the series, *Chain of Command*, earned Cooper the Marine Corps Heritage Foundation's prestigious James Webb Award in 2020.

While bouncing around the country in search of the perfect vacation (which is anywhere with his family), Cooper has called Nashville home since his final Marine duty station. When not enjoying the laid-back lifestyle of Music City, he's adding more novels to the list at www.cg-cooper.com.